THE RETURN OF CAPTAIN CONQUER

Borgo Press Books by MEL GILDEN

Dangerous Hardboiled Magicians
The Planetoid of Amazement: A Science Fiction Novel
The Return of Captain Conquer: A Science Fiction Novel

THE RETURN OF CAPTAIN CONQUER

A SCIENCE FICTION NOVEL

MEL GILDEN

THE BORGO PRESS
MMXI

This book is suitable for middle-grade readers.

THE RETURN OF CAPTAIN CONQUER

FIRST BORGO PRESS EDITION

Published by Wildside Press LLC

www.wildsidebooks.com

DEDICATION

For the man with forty pounds
of brains in his nose,

And his wife,
The smartest woman in the world.

CONTENTS

INTRODUCTION
"CAPTAIN CONQUER"

Though *The Return of Captain Conquer* was the first novel I had published, it was not the first one I wrote. In junior high school (what they now call middle school), I almost finished writing a fantasy novel called *The Golden Kazoo*. Running out of steam is normal for inexperienced writers, and I was no exception. It was many years before I tried the long form again.

One night I was at a party where most of the guests, me included, were science fiction fans. I was standing in the hallway discussing writing with a friend who knew even less about it than I did. We commiserated about what a long, difficult process writing a novel was, and we agreed that keeping the whole project in the air for a few hundred pages was nearly impossible. As I heard myself agreeing with this guy, I had my epiphany. I did not want to be like him. I would start another novel, and I would finish it. So there.

Thus began *The Electropomorphic Man*, a story about people who did surgery by recording a person on tape and then slicing out the lengths of tape they didn't want. (This was years before computers and compact disks were common. Recording on tape seemed pretty jazzy.) It was not a very good novel, nor was it very long (145 pages or so), but I did write the story out to the bitter end. Which was a triumph of sorts.

I wrote four more novels after that, each a little longer, and I think a little better, than the one before it. I learned that writing did not get easier, and the fact that I was typing on a manual typewriter did not help.

More years passed. I attended the Clarion Science Fiction Writers Workshop in Clarion, Pennsylvania, moved to the San Francisco Bay area, moved back to Los Angeles, and wrote short stories—a few of which I sold. I worked at the *Los Angeles Times* for three and a half years, became the editor of a magazine for people who collected antique slot machines, and, after a while, blindly joined a few of my friends in writing scripts for TV animation.

One of the shows I pitched to was called *The Getalong Gang*. It featured a sort of Our Gang/Little Rascals group made up of animals instead of kids. I thought it would be fun if the youngest of the Gang met her TV hero, and together they solved a big problem. Apparently, the people who owned the show disagreed with me because they rejected the premise.

However, the idea continued to nag at me. I thought the idea might make a novel, but I had no idea how to approach the material.

A few years before this I had been cohost of *Hour-25*, a radio program on which Mike Hodel and I interviewed anybody and everybody who had anything to do with speculative fiction. I even had a few fans. One of them sent me a copy of *The Snarkout Boys and the Avocado of Death* by Daniel Pinkwater. The book was both beautifully written and hilarious. It inspired me to get on the stick and write my TV hero novel.

Attempting to follow closely in Pinkwater's footsteps, I began to fiddle with the original cartoon premise, rearranging characters and situations. The gang of cute animals was one of the first things to go. I added a mixture of the heroes I watched on TV when I was a kid along with the products they sold and the mementoes they would send you in exchange for proof you had purchased their product and sometimes the investment of a quarter. Eventually I had an outline for the novel you hold in your hands. A few months after that I had my first draft.

One of the main characters in the book is the man with forty pounds of brains in his nose. And the book is dedicated to him and His Wife, The Smartest Woman in the World. The man with all the brains is my father. He always made the same claim I put into Fred Achziger's mouth. The smartest woman in the world is his wife, my mother. Who else? She was smart enough to marry him, wasn't she?

For a first-time author such as myself selling a novel can be difficult, more so without the help of an agent. I sent stacks of query letters to publishers and agents. Some answered back. Of those, most were not interested; a few agreed to have a look at my book.

Then one Saturday I got the letter of my dreams from Houghton Mifflin. They liked my book! They wanted to publish it!

Perhaps winning the World Series or the Super Bowl is comparable to the feeling one gets selling his or her first novel, but I am sure that few other life experiences come close to generating the high I felt that day—and for days after. Knowing very little about the publishing biz, I felt that I needed the guidance of an agent more than ever. And I figured that with a book contract in my metaphorical hand I could now get one. Nothing attracts the attention of an agent quicker than waving cash in her face.

On Monday morning I called one of the agents who had not yet rejected me and explained my situation. Sure enough she was delighted to hear from me. She went so far as to claim that she had been about to call *me*. It might even have been true.

When the book was released at last—or escaped, as my friends say—it got good reviews, but it was not the blockbuster I had hoped it would be. Still, very few conventions and book fairs pass without someone or two approaching me with a copy and asking for an autograph.

My agent and I tried to get the book reprinted in England, but the publishers over there misunderstood the title. They assumed that *Captain Conquer* was a real American TV show, and no one in the UK had ever seen it. No amount of explanation would change their minds.

A few years down the line a couple of independent movie producers suggested that they would be pleased to film *Captain Conquer* if there was a script. So I wrote a script. I did it less because I believed a movie would ever get made than because it gave me the opportunity to rethink a few items. For one, a fan pointed out that the book contained no major female characters. I was horrified to note that she was correct! So in the script I added a female friend for Watson Congruent. I also made Berkowitz the actor who'd played Destructowitz, rather than a prop man, adding more fun to the mix. Perhaps some day, if anybody cares, I will publish the script and you can compare the two versions yourself.

Little did I know that five years after the publication of *Captain Conquer* I would write a sequel called *The Planetoid of Amazement*, featuring Watson Congruent's son, Rodney.

—Mel Gilden
Los Angeles, California
April, 2011

CHAPTER ONE
THE HOUSE WITH
TWO FRONT DOORS

Well, this could be interesting, Watson Congruent thought hopefully. He stood behind the counter of the Captain Conquer PX, one hand resting on the cash register, watching the man at the other side of the room read the big cardboard sign that dangled on wires from the ceiling.

The man was not only Watson's sole customer, but he was also decked out in a really impressive Captain Conquer uniform. He wore a leather flight cap with goggles that he could pull down. A thin microphone reached on a wire arm from one ear hole and hung stiffly before his lips. His short khaki jacket had a Captain Conquer emblem on one shoulder and a Chocolatron emblem on the other. Medals covered his chest. Watson wondered what in the world he could have done to earn them. The man wore khaki pants that flared at the hips, but were skin tight as they went beneath his tall black boots.

The sign the man was looking at featured a big

glass of chocolate milk and a squat bottle filled with brown granules. The sign said in big futuristic letters:

DRINK CHOCOLATRON!
IT'S ATOM POWDERED!

"Wow," the man had said when he'd first entered the store. "We certainly don't have anything like this in Chicago." A nut, Watson thought. Certifiable. Just like all the other people who come into the Captain Conquer PX. If it weren't for guys like him, Watson thought, I would have gone crazy from boredom long ago.

Suddenly, from the back room came a loud screechy noise like that which might be made by a dying dinosaur. The man in the Captain Conquer suit looked around, then asked Watson, "What was that?"

Politely, Watson said, "That's my father."

"Your father?" the man exclaimed.

"Well, not actually my father himself, but his experiment. My father, the owner of this store, is trying to build a motivator like the one Captain Conquer used to power his stratoship, the Great Auk."

The man in the Captain Conquer suit looked at Watson suspiciously, as if trying to decide if what he had said was some kind of joke. "You're kidding," the man said.

"I'm afraid not."

"Pretty strange."

Watson nodded. Here was a man dressed as a TV hero who hadn't made a new show in twenty years telling Watson that something was strange. If you asked Watson, *that* was strange. Watson held up a sheet of paper and said, "Would you like to sign my father's petition demanding Harve Fishbein make a Captain Conquer feature film?"

"I certainly would," the man said, and strode across the wooden floor to the counter. While he signed his name, he said, "I wonder what happened to Fishbein after he made the last of the Conquer TV episodes."

"I couldn't say. Nobody even knows what happened to Webb Washington, the man who used to play Captain Conquer. Not even his agent, Alvin Algae, knows."

"Then who will you give the petition to?"

"We'll give it to Alvin Algae. He says he knows where Fishbein is, but he won't tell anybody. Can we help you with anything today?"

The man nodded and leaned across the counter as if he were telling Watson a secret. He said, "I'm looking for a genuine metal-tone styrene plastic Captain Conquer Signet Ring."

"Those rings are pretty rare. Chocolatron hasn't offered them as a premium since the show went off the air."

"I know. It's amazing how little respect people have for something they could get for five Chocolatron inner seals."

"We had one last week, but somebody bought it."

"How much was it?" The man braced himself.

"One hundred fifty dollars."

The man nodded and bit his lip.

Watson said, "We have replicas, and of course a lot of other stuff." He looked around at the Conquer PX. On the walls were posters of the Captain about to climb into the Great Auk, or talking to his side-kick, Chuckles. In bins under the posters were Conquer insignias and rank marks from all the seasons the show was on the air. A wire stand held fan publications and photocopies of new Captain Conquer stories written by enthusiasts who came into the PX all the time. In a big barrel in the center of the room were small pink plastic brains, like those the Captain found in the "Micro-Brains from the Penguin Star" episode. There were also model kits, coloring books, uniforms, and tape cassettes.

Watson thought all of this hero worship was pretty silly. He never would have taken a job in a place like this if the owner hadn't been his father.

"I dunno," the man said. "I really had my heart set on a genuine ring."

"Sorry."

The man strolled around the shop for a few more minutes, his boots making a clumping sound every time he put a foot down. At last he bought a pink micro-brain. Watson was glad to see him go.

Mr. Johnson, the mailman, came in pretty soon.

He was a nice old geezer, and Watson liked him. Mr. Johnson put down a stack of envelopes and said, "My granddaughter, Julia, has gone nutso over this Captain Conquer guy. She made me promise to buy her a poster of him and the Great Auk."

"How old is Julia?"

"Just turned twelve."

"Yeah, well, she's young yet."

Mr. Johnson chuckled. "Aren't you a fan?"

"Naw. My father is the fan in the family."

"Me neither. I used to watch *Captain Conquer* when it was first on. I never understood what all the shouting was about."

Watson got Mr. Johnson a rolled poster. He put it on the counter between them and said, "I tell you, Mr. Johnson, I'd believe in the Captain myself, if I could. Nothing exciting ever happens to me. I eat regularly. I have a warm place to sleep. I'm going crazy from being so secure. Sometimes I think I'll run away from home and pick peaches or something out in California."

"I don't think the Captain would recommend—" Mr. Johnson's words were suddenly cut off by a loud hammering noise coming from outside. The noise went on and on. Mr. Johnson and Watson looked at each other knowingly and shook their heads. Mr. Johnson paid for the poster, and Watson followed him to the door of the shop.

They stood there in the doorway watching a man from the Charlieville Department of Transportation pounding through the street asphalt with a jackhammer. A man sitting in the cab of a small steam shovel was watching him. Other men, leaning on shovels and rakes covered with tar, watched him too.

When the man stopped running his jackhammer for a moment, Watson said, "This sort of thing has been going on since I can remember. You'd think that after a while they'd get it right."

"Get what right?" said Mr. Johnson.

"Whatever they have to change under the street."

"Uh-oh," said Mr. Johnson as he gestured with his chin at a big black car driving up. "Here they come."

"They" was the Charlieville Planning Commission. A chauffeur dressed all in black, from his cap to his shiny boots, leaped out and opened the car door. It seemed to be a long time before the members of the Planning Commission emerged from the car.

They came out stiffly, one at a time. Each member of the Commission moved very slowly, as if he were older than anything. Each one stood at attention watching the roadwork and completely ignoring the difficulty the next Commissioner had getting out of the car.

Soon all five of them stood there in a row, like some kind of military unit. Each of them wore a black suit and a gleaming white shirt. On each head was a big slouch hat that flopped down around each set of ears. Each of them wore big impenetrable dark glasses. They folded their arms and watched the man with the jackhammer line up his next cut.

"I wonder why the Planning Commissioners always come out to watch the construction personally," said Watson.

"Don't trust anybody, I guess," said Mr. Johnson. "Maybe not even each other. Which is only one of the things that makes 'em look like the kind of bad guys that Captain Conquer might tangle with."

The Commissioners looked that way to Watson too. And oddly enough, if there was anything in the world to make him wish that Captain Conquer really existed, it was these five sinister men.

They had decided what the design of the city should be, what changes could and should be made. They seemed to be all-powerful, even when they made strange decisions, such as that a power pole should go in the middle of Mrs. Ferguson's back yard. The pole had been planted, wires had been strung, despite Mrs. Ferguson's logical protest that there was a perfectly good power pole already in use just fifteen feet away in the alley.

The jackhammer started again, so Watson just nodded. He waved at Mr. Johnson as he continued on his rounds. Watson went back inside the store.

Watson walked around the store, straightening things, sorting things back into their proper bins. It was his thirteenth birthday, and he suspected that his father would throw him a little party when that day's episode of *Captain Conquer* was over. There would be cake and ice cream and probably a present or two. Boring. Boring. Boring.

Watson stopped and looked into the display case that held some of the Captain Conquer toys his father had made from clothespins and cardboard and paper clips and string when Mr. Congruent was a kid. The cellophane tape was yellow and cracked, like a snake's shed skin, and the cardboard was discolored in spots. Mr. Congruent had never outgrown his interest. He was still a fan.

Watson shook his head. If Mom were there, she would never have let Dad indulge himself that way. Maybe Watson shouldn't either? No. As strange as this Captain Conquer stuff was, working with it made his father happy. And he wasn't really hurting anybody.

The dying dinosaur noise began again. It competed with the jackhammer noise from outside. If Watson was inclined to get headaches, this two-part musical invention for motivator and jackhammer would certainly give him one. Watson stood behind the counter with one hand on the cash register.

Suddenly, both noises stopped at once. In the silence, Watson heard somebody knocking energetically on the door, but not the door to the shop.

The Captain Conquer PX was located in the house where Watson and his father lived. There were two doors at the front of the house—one for their living quarters and one for the store. Big signs pointed out the store. Most people were not confused. The fact that the wrong door was being knocked on tipped Watson off as to who was doing the knocking.

Watson walked to the door of the shop and looked out. There, knocking with increasing anger on the door to their private living quarters, was a short man puffing on the stub of a cigar. He wore a coat and pants of conflicting plaids, and a bow tie that looked like an Amazonian butterfly. He stopped knocking for a moment to push his black-rimmed glasses up on his nose.

"In here, Mr. Algae," Watson called.

Alvin Algae looked at Watson in surprise, then strutted to the shop door, waggling his finger at him. "I don't know how you expect to do any business if you keep your front door locked."

"That's the door to our private living quarters. *This* is the door to the store." Watson attempted to speak patiently, though he had told Alvin Algae, Webb Washington's agent, which door was which many times.

Alvin Algae bustled past Watson as the street noise started again. It was soon joined by the sound of Mr. Congruent's experiment in the back room. Alvin Algae stood in the middle of the shop tapping his foot, looking around as if he'd just bought the place and was thinking of turning it into a parking lot. "Can't you stop that noise?"

Alvin Algae shouted.

"I'm not making it," Watson shouted back, trying to be troublesome without being impolite.

Alvin Algae walked nervously around the room, picking up things, then putting them down without looking at them. He stopped under the Chocolatron sign and said, "Did you get any signatures?"

"A few."

"Let me see." He held out his hand and waited.

Watson picked up the petition and walked across the floor to hand it to Alvin Algae. Algae took it and glared at it as if it were an enemy. "Only fifteen," he said angrily.

"Some people don't want to sign because nobody knows where Webb Washington is and they can't imagine anybody else playing Captain Conquer."

"I'll find him when the time comes. I told you that."

"A lot of people think that if you could find him, you'd have done it by now."

"Excuses!" Alvin Algae cried. The jackhammer stopped, leaving the odd cry of Mr. Congruent's experiment hanging in the air like a torn scarf. "Excuses," Alvin Algae said a little more quietly. "I want to talk to your father."

"Sure," said Watson, and then called out, "Hey, Dad. Somebody wants to see you."

"Heck of a way to treat your father," Alvin Algae said.

"We understand each other."

Soon the noise coming from the back room stopped, and seconds later Mr. Congruent pushed the dull green curtain aside and entered the shop.

Watson's father was a small man with a small protruding tummy that made him look as if he'd swallowed a basketball. He had short sandy hair that stuck out every which way from the top of his head. But his face was pleasant, and usually wore a smile. He put out his hand to Alvin Algae and said, "Nice to see you again, Alvin."

"I wish that I could say the same, Sherlock. Your son tells me that you've collected only fifteen signatures since I was here last."

"Then I'm sure it's true. Watson wouldn't lie."

"I'm sure he wouldn't, but that's not the point. The point is that more signatures will be needed to convince Harve Fishbein to make the movie."

"It's difficult to get signatures when nobody knows where either Fishbein or Webb Washington is. Perhaps the man with forty pounds of brains in his nose could be of help. If you'd like to come with me to the retirement party that Channel Fourteen is throwing for him on Monday, you can ask him. When he's no longer working for the TV station he should have plenty of time."

"Ha," said Alvin Algae. "Forty pounds of brains, indeed. Money will get you through times of no brains better than brains will get you through times of no money."

"You ought to know," Sherlock Congruent said.

"You're the one with the money. Would you like to stay to see today's *Captain Conquer* episode? It'll be on in a few minutes and we have a TV set right in the back room."

Alvin Algae curled his lip and said, "I never watch that stuff. It's enough that I had to keep track of Webb Washington's business without having to watch him act." He carefully creased the petition and put it into his pocket. He shook his fist at Sherlock Congruent and said, "Captain Conquer will return, with or without your help."

When Alvin Algae was gone, Mr. Congruent said, "Somehow, you know, I think he's right."

"What makes you think so?" said Watson.

"I've had some interest shown in my motivator. But I don't want to talk about that now. Today's *Captain Conquer* episode is about to begin."

CHAPTER TWO
A RING AS BIG AS A WALNUT

Watson hung a sign on the shop's door that said BACK AT 4:30, then ducked around the green curtain after his father. The back room was dim but for the gooseneck lamp that reached over the workbench, and it was crowded with the same stuff that was displayed in the PX, but not stored as neatly.

Watson followed his father along the narrow path of blue carpeting between the jumbled piles of posters and T-shirts to the back of the room, where Mr. Congruent's workshop was located.

The workshop was even messier than the rest of the room. Revealed on the workbench by the light coming from the gooseneck lamp, standing among bits of wire, circuit boards and tools, was an oscilloscope that showed a strange curve that shuddered and re-formed time and time again on the round green screen. Big circuit diagrams smudged with clouds of fingerprints covered the walls.

Near the oscilloscope, a finely machined piece of equipment stood on the bench. It looked something like an electric fan, but the round part where the blades might have been was completely encased in metal. A plate had been unscrewed from its side, and alligator clips clamped wires to blocky shapes inside. The wires led from the electric-fan-like thing to the oscilloscope.

Watson watched the oscilloscope for a few seconds.

"How's the motivator coming?"

Mr. Congruent carefully inserted a long thin screwdriver down into the motivator's exposed innards. "Oh, I'm pretty close now." They watched the luminous line on the screen of the oscilloscope wriggle while Mr. Congruent turned the screwdriver slowly, first one way and then the other.

Mr. Congruent put down the screwdriver, then spun a lazy Susan that stood on one corner of the bench. A television set swung into view. Watson switched it on, and adjusted the sound on the Corny Cobs commercial that was on the screen, then sat in a big raggedy overstuffed chair next to the one in which his father was already sitting.

As the jaunty march music that was the theme of *The Adventures of Captain Conquer* began, and clips of Captain Conquer taking off in the Great Auk, thwarting bad guys and shaking hands with Chuckles, his assistant, rolled across the screen, Mr. Congruent leaned forward expectantly in his chair. When the words "The Attack of the Proto-Penguins" flashed on the screen, he said, "Oh, I remember this. This is a good one."

Watson was not surprised at his father's words. Mr. Congruent rarely said anything else when he saw the title of each day's episode.

Mr. Congruent studied his fingers and picked at his thumb while the first Chocolatron commercial was on. He said, "I wish they were still giving premiums. I'll bet a lot of people would want an authentic metal-tone styrene plastic Captain Conquer Signet Ring. Or a model of the Great Auk, or a Chuckles activity book. After all, when you're a Captain Conquer fan, you're a member of a big happy family. Don't you agree, Watson?"

"It's nice to think so," Watson said. His family had consisted of just his father and himself for so long that the possibility of being a member of a big happy family made Watson feel warm and wistful.

"Yes," said Mr. Congruent, "I've said it before and I'll say it again: 'Fandom is a way of life'."

Soon "The Attack of the Proto-Penguins" began. Mr. Congruent instantly stopped playing with his fingers, leaned forward and followed with interest the story of android penguins from the ice floes of Venus. When Captain Conquer spoke, Mr. Congruent paid attention as if the Captain were speaking directly to him.

He nodded when Captain Conquer wisely did not use weapons until the true nature of the penguins and their mission was discovered. As it turned out, the penguins were programmed by the evil Destructowitz to explode if attacked. If the Captain had fired at them, as so many of his advisers wanted him to, the laboratory and half the mountain it sat on would have been blown to smithereens.

Mr. Congruent laughed at the antics of Chuckles as he tried to free himself from the evil Destructowitz's quicksand field. He shook his head and groaned when Captain Conquer was captured by the evil Destructowitz.

During the next Chocolatron commercial, Watson handed the mail to his father. One of the letters was from the Charlieville Planning Commission.

"At last," Mr. Congruent said as he tore open the envelope and started to read the thin sheet of paper inside. He stopped smiling as he continued.

"What is it?" Watson said.

"The Planning Commission has denied our request to build a Captain Conquer Museum next door."

"Can they do that?" Watson said hotly. "They don't own the land. We do." Watson's sense of honor was often offended by the Charlieville Planning Commission.

"It says here that building on that land would violate certain city zoning ordinances and planning policies." Mr. Congruent angrily balled up the paper and threw it to Watson, who smoothed out the paper on his knee and read the legal language with disbelief. Yes, it did seem to say what his father claimed, though only a lawyer could be sure.

"I wish they would write these things in English, don't you?" Watson said. Mr. Congruent did not answer, for suddenly, there on the television, Captain Conquer was once again in the clutches of the evil Destructowitz and Mr. Congruent once more became engrossed in the story. He seemed to have entirely forgotten how angry he was at the Planning Commission.

Watson knew it was impossible to distract his father while *The Adventures of Captain Conquer* was on. He folded the letter from the Planning Commission and stuffed it back into its envelope.

Things got worse for Captain Conquer. Ravenous proto-penguins attacked seafood restaurants all over the Earth, ate out their freezers, put everyone of them out of business. People who frequented sushi bars could not get enough raw fish, and were rioting in the streets.

Just before the proto-penguins were about to dive into the ocean to eat everything that swam or crawled, Captain Conquer wriggled out of the ropes holding him and got to the Great Auk. He flew over the crowd of proto-penguins and dropped a powder that reduced them to their component organic molecules. The evil Destructowitz escaped back to Venus, vowing revenge. As he flew into the sunset, Captain Conquer spoke the famous line he said to Chuckles at the end of every show: "So much for that mess!"

Mr. Congruent shook his head in wonderment.

"Wasn't that swell?" he said.

"Swell. Yeah," said Watson with all the enthusiasm he could muster.

The same Corny Cobs commercial they had seen at the beginning of the show was running again.

"Well," said Mr. Congruent as he hit his knees with the palms of his hands and stood up, "I think it's time for a little celebration."

"What sort of celebration?" Watson asked innocently.

Mr. Congruent opened a cupboard above his workbench and took a cake from it and displayed it before Watson. "It's your birthday!" he said. The cake was really a package of Twinkies. Thirteen candles, each in a pink plastic candleholder, had been punched through the cellophane and into the yellow cakes.

"Gee," Watson said happily.

Mr. Congruent lit the candles, and with one huge breath, Watson blew them out. They removed the candles and opened the package of Twinkies. Mr. Congruent said, "Let's get outside that cake!" Mr. Congruent never "ate" anything. He always "got outside" it. He and Watson each had a Twinkie with vanilla ice cream on a little paper plate. They had big glasses of cold milk and Chocolatron to wash it down.

As they got outside their cake, ice cream, and Chocolatron, Watson and his father joked and laughed. Mr. Congruent mentioned how proud his wife would have been of a fine young man such as

Watson.

When they were done eating, Mr. Congruent threw away the paper plates and plastic forks. Watson said, "Thanks for the birthday party, Dad. I enjoyed it a lot." He stood up. "Well, I guess we'd better get back to work."

"The store will wait, Watson. We'll hear the bell over the door tinkle if someone comes in. I have a little something for you on your birthday." From a pocket, he pulled a small white box.

"Jewelry?" Watson said. He and Mr. Congruent laughed and Mr. Congruent handed him the box. "I suppose it is jewelry of a sort. You're old enough to use it properly now."

Trying to make the surprise last longer, Watson slowly pulled off the top of the box. Inside was a mound of cotton. Beneath the cotton was a bulbous hunk of plastic about the size of a walnut. It was connected to a plastic ring. On the surface of the hunk of plastic, Watson could see a tiny compass and a chip of mirror. The thing that Watson held in his hand was not something that he had expected. He didn't know whether to laugh or cry.

"It's a Captain Conquer Signet Ring," Watson said evenly.

"Yes, indeed," Mr. Congruent said proudly. "And it is not one of those replicas. It is a genuine metal -tone styrene plastic Captain Conquer Signet Ring that I got for five inner seals from Chocolatron when I was about your age. Do you like it?"

"It's a real surprise," Watson said.

"Well, I figure that I won't be around forever, and you'll need something like that in case you ever get into some really big trouble. The ring has many secret features that might come in handy." Mr. Congruent spent the next half hour explaining all the features of the ring. Watson smiled and nodded, though he'd been familiar with Captain Conquer rings since he could remember, and could have as easily demonstrated the ring to Mr. Congruent.

"Here," said Mr. Congruent, handing the ring back, "let's see how it looks on you."

Watson took the ring, but he held it gingerly, as if he were holding a live stinging insect. "Uh, maybe later, Dad. I have to go back to work now."

"Don't worry about that. We'll hear the bell. Put it on." When Watson still hesitated, Mr. Congruent said, "Is there something wrong?"

Watson shrugged. "I don't know."

"Tell me about it," Mr. Congruent said.

Watson looked at the toes of his shoes. "I...well... that is, you see, Dad, most of the kids in school don't understand about Captain Conquer."

Mr. Congruent was genuinely puzzled. "What's not to understand?" he said.

Watson turned the ring over and over in his hand. "Well, most of them never heard of him. And the ones who have heard of him think he's just for kids."

"Just for kids? The greatest Force for Good on

Earth?"

"Dad," Watson said softly, "it's comforting to know that the fans Captain Conquer does have all stick together and help each other. But aside from the good that comes from fandom being a way of life, Captain Conquer is not a force for anything, except maybe Chocolatron."

"I see."

"The kids already think I'm strange because my name is Watson and your name is Sherlock. I have Sherlock Holmes jokes coming out of my ears. I don't know what some of the kids will do if I show up at school wearing this ring."

Except for the sound of the crew digging up the street outside, the back room of the Captain Conquer PX was silent. Watson and Mr. Congruent could not look at each other.

Mr. Congruent sighed and said, "Are you ashamed of your old man?"

Watson looked up suddenly. "What? Of course not. Don't be silly."

"Then wear the ring. If anybody asks, tell 'em you're a member of the Conquer Corps."

"You really think that'll help?"

"I'm sure of it."

Watson looked from the ring in his hand to his father's expectant face. He saw that argument would lead only to bad feelings and frustration. His father would never understand that not everybody shared his enthusiasm for Captain Conquer. It was sometimes futile to argue with adults.

Watson decided that he would have to figure something out for himself. Besides, it couldn't hurt to wear the ring around the store. He could tell himself that it was good for business.

Watson slipped the ring onto his finger. Mr. Congruent smiled and clapped him on the shoulder. They each went back to work.

* * * * * * *

On Monday morning, Watson walked out the front door of the private living quarters of the house, ready for school and wearing the Captain Conquer Signet Ring. There had been no way to avoid it.

As Watson dawdled toward the bus stop, a plan took shape in his head. As he had expected, he was alone when he got to the bus stop. Feeling silly for feeling guilty, Watson slipped the ring off his finger, and slid it into his pocket. For a few minutes his finger felt cold and empty, as his legs might feel if he'd forgotten to wear his pants. But by the time the bus came, he felt a lot better and did not need to hide his hands.

When he arrived at Casablanca Junior High School, he strolled through the crowded corridors to his locker as casually as he could, knowing what he carried in his pocket. He opened his locker, and like a magician attempting to show by his nonchalance how unimportant was the wave of his hand, Watson pulled the ring from his pocket and threw it into the locker.

The ring rebounded from the back of the locker

with a boom, bounced off his algebra book, and rolled across the floor of the corridor. Perhaps thinking it was a mouse, students backed out of the way of the ring's flight—some of them squealing with surprise—until it was picked up by a hulking football player that Watson shared an English class with. The fellow's name was Pemberton, and Watson was of the opinion that Pemberton was lucky to understand English, let alone speak it.

Pemberton held the Captain Conquer Signet Ring up to his eyes with a big meaty paw and blinked at it. "Hey, Congruent, what is this thing?"

"It's a ring," Watson said, and grabbed for it.

Pemberton pulled the ring away and continued to study it. "Hey, I know what it is," he said with the joy of a caveman finding a particularly tasty louse in his hair, "it's one-a them Captain Concourse rings! Hey, Maxwell," he called to one of his gridiron friends, "lookit this!" He winked at three girls who stood together in the crowd that had gathered, and threw the ring to Maxwell. Watson dashed after it.

"Hiya, Watson, solve any good crimes lately?" Maxwell laughed at his own wit. Somewhere, he had read a comic book about Sherlock Holmes, and his knowledge was forever a source of irritation for Watson. Watson tried to grab the ring as Maxwell tossed and caught it in one hand. Maxwell threw the ring back to Pemberton.

Pemberton caught the ring easily in one hand and the girls sighed. He said, "My little sister watches this crap. She says she knows your old man, Congruent. Says he's some kinda weird guy." He held the ring out of reach while Watson stood with his arms folded and glared at him.

The bell rang for first period. Pemberton tossed the Captain Conquer ring at Watson and said, "Stay outa trouble, Captain," and iaughed as he and Maxwell and two cheerleaders walked off together.

The ring dropped. at Watson's feet, and he had to scramble among rapidly moving legs, following it as it was kicked and spun this way and that and as it ricocheted along the corridor. He hoped the styrene plastic could stand up under this kind of punishment.

Even before he took a good look at the ring, Watson could feel that it was broken. It was cracked along one seam, and a big triangular shard was missing. Worst of all, the little mirror was cracked. Certainly, nothing could follow now but bad luck.

Wondering what he would.tell his father, Watson carefully buried the ring beneath some stiff fragrant sweat socks that had been in the back of his locker for two semesters, then walked off to his biology class hoping that nobody who knew him had seen his adventure with Pemberton and Maxwell.

Watson needn't have worried because the two football players had spread the story of his humiliation all over the school. Even his physical education teacher called him Captain Concourse once.

There was no relief even when he was alone, because Watson had to think about what he would tell his father, and what his father would say, and how awful both of them would feel. It was a terrible day.

On the bus ride home, Watson opened his history book and pretended to be studying. But all he saw before him was his father's disappointed face.

However, the day at school was nothing compared to what life was like when Watson got home. To begin with, traffic was snarled when he got off the bus, and it got worse as he walked toward his house. The Department of Transportation work crew had gone, but they had left behind yellow sawhorses straddling the open trenches they had dug into the street. People honked and shouted nasty things at each other as they tried to steer slowly by in their cars.

Watson watched the traffic for as long as he could, then he sighed. He could not put off forever telling his father that the ring was broken. But when he turned to look at the house with two front doors, he found nothing but a path leading up to an empty dirt plot where his house had once been.

CHAPTER THREE
THE AMAZING USELESS RING

Watson gaped at the empty lot for a long time, no longer hearing the traffic noise behind him. Then slowly, like someone in shock, for indeed that was what he was, Watson walked forward. He stopped when his toes reached the end of the path, when they reached the place where the first step up into the house should have been. Was the space beyond radioactive? Enchanted? Contagious? What?

The place where the house had been was now just an empty rectangle of ground. The dirt was lumpy, as if somebody had dragged a tiller through it. (Though Watson was a city boy, he had once seen a tiller in a movie about farm life.) Not even weeds were growing on the lot yet. After all, the house had still been there this morning.

Watson walked slowly through the big tilled rectangle of dirt, turning clods over with his foot, looking, he imagined, for clues. While he did this, he thought about the official metal-tone styrene plastic Captain Conquer Signet Ring. His father had told him that the ring would come in handy during emergencies.

This was certainly an emergency. He went over all the features possessed by the broken ring, looking for one that might be useful at this time.

The ring included an emergency light, a coil of string (which the Chocolatron people called rope), a whistle, a tiny mirror, a combination magnifying glass/telescope, a compass, a deck of playing cards that was barely bigger than his thumbnail, a message decoder, a pencil, a signet (for embossing secret documents), a clicker, a knife, and a secret compartment.

Try as he might, Watson could not see how any of this stuff could be useful to him in his present bad situation. He was amazed by this, but the fact that the ring was totally useless in an emergency made him feel better about its being broken.

Watson kicked aside yet another clod of dirt and revealed something that glinted in the slanting afternoon sunshine. Maybe it was a clue! Watson picked it up and saw that it was another Captain Conquer Signet Ring. But it was heavier than the ring he'd gotten for his birthday. As a matter of fact, Watson was astonished to find that the ring was made of metal.

The metal-tone styrene plastic rings were all really toys. The emergency light was really just a knob of plastic that glowed in the dark for a while after you held it up to light; the compass was a shred of tin stuck on a pin. Everything else was made of plastic, and was small, and would probably fall apart after the average kid used it a few times.

But all the features on the ring that Watson found

in the empty lot worked. The emergency light glowed so brightly that Watson could see it even in daylight; the compass looked waterproof, like something a commando might expect to get a lot of rough use out of in a jungle or swamp; the knife was sharp; the rope was made of some kind of fiber that Watson could not break even when he tried as hard as he could.

In the fingerhole of the ring was a balled-up piece of paper. Watson smoothed it out and saw that it was the letter he and his father had received from the Charlieville Planning Commission. This was definitely a clue, but Watson didn't know what to make of it. He turned the piece of paper over and his eyes widened.

For on the other side of the paper was a message that looked like this:

ZPGLE ZCPIMUGRX RM
AYNRYGL AMLOSCPQ JYZ.

Watson had no idea what that meant, but it was obviously some kind of code. He guessed that the code could probably be broken using the Captain Conquer decoder. Maybe the ring wasn't useless after all. Watson shook his head, and mentally kicked himself because he had never bothered to learn the Captain's decoding methods.

Watson looked at the decoder now. After all, he was a bright kid. The ring was designed to be used by kids a lot dumber than he was. How difficult could it be?

The decoder was a flat dial that swung out of the ring on a pivot. Pinned to the center of the dial was an arrow with one point pointing one way, and three more points pointing generally in the other direction.

"Well," Watson said to himself as he sat down on the path to study the decoder. He held the ring in his hands and kept the paper from blowing away with one foot. He was ready to attempt decoding the message when the enormity of what had happened struck him for the first time.

It was all very well to say that his house was gone, and his father with it. But even with the evidence before him, the fact was difficult to believe. It was only when Watson sat down to figure out what had happened that his eyes filled with tears and he felt terribly empty and alone. Through his tears, the Captain Conquer ring looked like a gray blob. He sniffled, and could not think straight for a long time.

After what seemed to be hours of just sitting, thinking about how miserable he was, Watson heard a siren approaching. He looked up.

Out in the street, cars were turning every which way, trying to get over to the side. But there wasn't much room, and they smashed into each other like Dodg'em cars at an amusement park. The cars were all moving so slowly that nobody was hurt, but people got out and stood around in angry little knots, arguing about whose fault what accident was.

Then, still blowing its siren, a black limousine careened around the corner and down the crowded street. Watson watched as it maneuvered between the smaller cars like a shark among goldfish, and was astonished when it stopped in front of his house. Or rather, in front of the place where his house used to be. He sniffled.

Watson had recovered enough from his shock and his depression to shove the ring and the message into his pocket. He didn't want just anybody to know about them. He had to think things over first.

A chauffeur dressed all in black ran around to open the back door of the limousine, and one by one, the members of the Charlieville Planning Commission emerged.

Watson was actually glad to see them. They were officials of the city. They would help him figure out what had happened, and help him find his father.

Walking stiffly, the five Commissioners approached him. Watson stood up. The dark glasses and floppy hats did not give the Commissioners an encouraging look. Still, Watson said, "Boy, am I glad to see you guys."

"Why?" one of the Commissioners said. Watson could not tell which one.

"Because my father is gone," Watson cried. Hot tears rolled down his cheeks again, leaving cold tracks. "And somebody has stolen our house!"

One of the Commissioners said, "What did you

do with the house? We never gave you permission to move a house."

Another Commissioner said, "And why have you kidnapped your father?"

Watson was so surprised by these questions that he stopped crying and just stared at the Commissioners. He didn't know what to say.

Another Commissioner (or was it the same one?) said, "If you don't speak to us, you will have to speak with the police. They will be here soon. Hear the siren?"

Watson could, in fact, hear a siren. It was still far away, but it was getting closer.

"Sure. Well. You guys are crazy, you know?" Watson had never before accused a city official of being crazy—not to his face, anyway—but he felt justified in this case. "I'll find my house and my father myself." He ran down the path, eager to get away before the police arrived.

"After him!" shouted one of the Commissioners.

As Watson rounded the front of the limousine, the chauffeur leaped from where he had been polishing the hood with his sleeve and ran after him. Watson dodged through the heavy traffic around the street construction. Horns honked and tires squealed. The chauffeur reached for Watson, but Watson ducked under one of the construction crew's sawhorses and jumped into the trench they had dug that day. He looked back as he ran through the wet gravel at the bottom of the trench, and saw that the chauffeur was looking at him from outside the fence of sawhorses, but making no attempt to follow him. Watson ran under a sidewalk that bridged the trench and found himself inside a big drainpipe.

It was dark inside the pipe and the pipe was not large enough to allow him to stand up all the way. Crouching, he pulled the ring from his pocket and switched on its emergency light. In the sudden bright illumination, Watson could see the water-stained walls that curved to make a ceiling above and a floor below. A trickle of water ran down the center of the floor, and Watson splashed through it as he walked.

Walking bent over was uncomfortable. After a while he was stiff and his back hurt. The place smelled like dead things and dirt, and sometimes, among the echoes of his own movement, Watson heard skitterings that he was sure were made by rats. He was cold, as if he were hundreds of miles underground. Watson watched for a ladder or something that would let him out of there.

He walked straight ahead, though pipes occasionally led off to the side. He figured that he would get less lost that way. Sometimes he stopped and listened for sounds of pursuit, but there were none, only the skitterings of rats.

Then, up ahead, Watson saw the ladder he had hoped for. He slid the Captain Conquer ring onto a finger and climbed up the dark shaft.

Moments later, Watson reached a metal ceiling.

Through a hole in the ceiling, he could see the sky and hear traffic noise. He decided that the ceiling must be a manhole cover, and he pushed up on it as hard as he could. He slid the heavy metal lid to one side with a wet, gritty sound, and let in sunlight. The traffic noise got louder. He must have been far from where he'd started because this traffic sounded free-flowing and happy.

Watson pulled himself out of the manhole and found himself sitting on the yellow line in the center of Perry Boulevard, a big main street with cars rushing by and big stores on both sides. He waited until the traffic thinned, then ran across the street to April Limited, the biggest department store in town.

Inside April Limited the air was cool. With the big crowded air-conditioned building around him, Watson felt safe from the Planning Commission. Near the door, he made a little puddle wherever he put his foot down. That soon stopped, though his wet shoes continued to make squishing sounds as he wandered around the store. His feet were cold and itchy. Watson was worried that he would catch pneumonia any minute.

In the shoe department, Watson sat for a while to gather his forces and think about what he would do next. A shoe salesman stared at him for a moment, but did not seem interested in chasing him away. Actually he did not seem interested in much of anything except the book he was reading, *Investing in Penguin Belly Futures for Fun and Profit.*

Watson found that in addition to the Captain Conquer Signet Ring—which had turned out to be more useful than he'd thought possible—he had almost a dollar in change. He needed help. The best way to spend that money was on a phone call. But to whom?

While Watson sat there, a security guard walked by. Watson got up and walked casually from the shoe department in the other direction, feeling like some kind of criminal.

Watson was angry about that; he was no criminal. He had always kind of liked policemen, though he had never really had much to do with them. The fact that the Planning Commission probably held a sinister control over the police had given him a new attitude, and Watson was not pleased about that. He did not like being a fugitive.

He found a telephone and looked at it. He fingered the change in his pocket for a moment, then put a dime into the slot, dialed, and waited while the number rang. Then, over the phone, he heard: "Congratulations! You have reached the Alvin Algae Agency, talent representatives for motion pictures and television. No one is here right now, but if you'll leave your name, your number...."

Watson listened to the end of the recorded message, and hung up. He needed help right now, not whenever Alvin Algae might pick up his messages. Besides, where could Alvin Algae call him back, even if he was inclined to do so? And the police, under the Planning Commission's control, would do more harm than good. There was only one thing that Watson could do. He would have to call Captain Conquer.

Wasn't Watson's problem as unlikely as many of those he'd seen the Captain solve? Someone (or something?) had kidnapped both his house and his father. That was not exactly a normal crime.

And Mr. Congruent had always told Watson that Captain Conquer's fans were like members of a big family, that fandom was a way of life. The time had come for Watson to find out if his father's comforting theory was true.

Yes, Watson would go to Captain Conquer for help. And Watson knew just the place to start looking for him.

* * * * * * *

Channel 14 had been running *The Adventures of Captain Conquer* every weekday, almost since the first-run episodes went off the air. More important, Watson knew that the man with forty pounds of brains in his nose worked there, or would until his retirement. Maybe Watson could talk to him at his retirement party.

The station's offices were in a low gray building with advertisements for its shows on billboards all over the top of it. "Watch *Turn the Tables*!" "See *The Flackdoodle Show*!" "Visit *The Ackermans*!" Watson had never seen these shows, but he knew that they were all either game shows or twenty-year-old situation comedies.

Watson walked the short distance between April Limited and Channel 14, feeling self-conscious about his appearance. He was still dirty from his journey through the drains, and his shoes, now dry, felt as if they were made of cardboard. The fact that he had nowhere to go and change clothes, he felt, would make little difference to the grown-ups he would meet.

Worse than that, he had no idea what to say. A thirteen-year-old kid who walks into a TV station and asks to see a guy who never existed outside a soundstage, and hasn't even existed *there* for twenty years, can expect some strange looks and a quick brush-off. The response would probably be even worse if Watson asked to see a man he knew only as the man with forty pounds of brains in his nose. Watson wished he knew the man's real name.

But people did have an interest in Captain Conquer or his reruns would not be on the air. Somebody at the station must be used to answering questions about him. That person might be the man with forty pounds of brains in his nose. Watson would ask questions about Captain Conquer rather than ask to see him. That, certainly, was the approach to take.

Armed with a plan, Watson pulled open one of the glass double doors. The security guard glanced up from his magazine as Watson mounted the wide stairs to a big shiny lobby that he crossed to confront the receptionist. She was seated in a booth against the far wall. Watson looked over the counter at the pretty dark-haired woman wearing a telephone head set. He heard her say, "Channel Fourteen, good afternoon." She sounded happy, but she looked bored.

When the receptionist stopped talking into the microphone of her headset and looked at Watson he said, "Hi! I'm with the Casablanca Junior High *Daily Letters of Transit*—you know, the school paper?—and I'm writing an article about Captain Conquer. Is there anybody here I can talk to about him?"

The receptionist said, "Nobody in Publicity is available right now, but I can give you these." She spoke fast, as if she'd said all this before. She selected four sheets of paper from a set of trays nearby, and handed them to Watson. Her switchboard lit up. She got a faraway look in her eyes as she turned away from Watson and said, "Channel Fourteen, good afternoon...."

Watson took the papers she had given to him, and sat down in a chrome and leather chair in a row of chairs at one side of the lobby. The lobby was very quiet. The traffic outside passed like the ghost of traffic. The only sounds in the place were the rustle of the security guard turning magazine pages, the soft voice of the receptionist as she answered the phone and the hiss of the air conditioning. The Planning Commission seemed very far away.

The first sheet was titled, "Webb Washington *IS* Captain Conquer," and it was a biography of Webb Washington. Watson read it through. Not much help there. Nobody knew where Webb Washington was.

The second sheet was titled, "The Secret Origin of Captain Conquer." This told briefly about the Captain's war experiences, and how he'd inherited this huge fortune and how he'd decided to use his intellectual and financial resources to fight crime. Watson could tell that it was all made-up stuff. Not much help with a real problem.

The third sheet was titled, "The Adventures of Captain Conquer," and was a list of all the shows. The fourth sheet was all about how good Chocolatron was for you.

Watson shook his head as he folded the sheets and put them into his pocket. Dejected, he left the building. He stood in front of Channel 14 wondering what he would do next. It was getting dark. He would have to find food and a place to sleep. He pulled the change from his pocket and counted it. Seventy-eight cents. He could not get much of a dinner for that, and breakfast would be a real problem.

Watson smelled food. He followed his nose around the corner, and saw a line of men and women dressed as waiters picking up big cloth-covered trays from a man in a panel truck and running onto the Channel 14 lot. Somebody was having a party. Watson hoped that it was the retirement party of the man with forty pounds of brains in his nose. After all, how many parties could Channel 14 throw on the average Monday afternoon? Even if it was not the right party, Watson could probably get something to eat there.

Watson brushed himself off, spruced himself up as best he could, and walked to the panel truck.

The man in the truck was rummaging around among napkins and silverware. When he heard Watson approaching the man hollered, "Take it! Take it!" without even turning around. Watson picked up one of the big cloth-covered aluminum trays that was sitting on the curb and followed the other waiters through the gate. The guard just nodded at him.

CHAPTER FOUR
FORTY POUNDS OF
BRAINS IN HIS NOSE

The waiter in front of Watson walked very fast, and Watson could barely keep up, carrying his heavy tray. Watson's mouth watered at the wonderful meaty smells that blew back into his face. He walked faster so that he wouldn't have to wait much longer before he could put the tray down and eat some of what was under the cloth.

Watson followed the other waiters through a doorway that could have let in an elephant with no trouble. Next to the doorway in big black letters were the words SOUNDSTAGE ONE.

The room beyond was one of the biggest places Watson had ever seen in his life. Once, he'd gone to Chicago with his father to see about opening a Captain Conquer PX branch there. They had walked around a hotel called the Palahnuk Towers. It was really just a big hollow shell, with rooms going up on all sides of the lobby for fifty floors, so the lobby was fifty floors high. Elevators crawled up and down the walls right out where you could see them.

Birds lived in big trees that grew right up out of the floor. It was a pretty spectacular place.

Though Soundstage One was not as tall as the lobby of the Palahnuk Towers, it was at least the size of two baseball diamonds. Running just beneath the ceiling, which had to be at least two stories high, were catwalks and banks of lights and tied-up hanks of thick rope. A few men were up on a catwalk leaning on the rail, watching the activity below. Each of them held a white Styrofoam cup from which he occasionally took a sip. Hanging from the ceiling was a big hand-painted banner that said GOOD LUCK, FRED!!!

Watson set his tray on a long white table that extended halfway along one wall of the soundstage. He then walked off and lost himself in the crowd.

There were men in suits, and women in fancy dresses covered with spangles. But there were also people in T-shirts and jeans who weren't much more dressed up than Watson, though he had to admit they were cleaner. Everybody was talking and laughing and having a good time. The place was so big that all the noise seemed to float away and get lost up near the ceiling. Watson decided that nobody would notice him if he was careful.

The most important thing, as far as Watson was concerned, was that almost everybody was carrying a little paper plate piled with food. He strolled back to the long white table and picked up a plate. One of the big trays was filled with rare roast beef; another was filled with slices of turkey; a third had little sandwiches and pickles and olives. Watson walked down the line, piling his plate high, and then strolled back out into the crowd to eat.

He hadn't eaten since lunch, and he'd had a lot of surprises and exercise since then. He was very hungry. The food tasted good and he scarfed it down as he strolled. He noticed that the man standing under the banner seemed to be the focus of the party.

The man was old and thin with a great wave of thick white hair swept back from his forehead. If he'd been a bird, he would have been an eagle. He was dressed in a purple suit and matching tie that looked almost as if they were glowing. People were coming up to him, congratulating him, shaking his hand. Some of the women kissed him. Every time a woman kissed him, he turned bright red, but he smiled at her just the same.

The thing that Watson liked best about the old guy was that he recognized him. The old guy was one of the fans of Captain Conquer who used to visit his father all the time. He must be the man with forty pounds of brains in his nose. Which was funny because though the man's nose was flat and hooked, Watson had seen much bigger ones on just regular people in the street. He didn't remember the man's name, but he guessed it was Fred.

Watson could not get close to Fred because of all the grown-ups who were in the way, so he tried to attract Fred's attention by waving to him. All he succeeded in doing was making himself conspicuous to a massive old woman who looked at him through a pair of glasses that she held up to her eyes on a stick.

Watson stopped and tried to think. Thinking was easier now that he had gotten outside some food. He frowned when he thought about how his father used to say that. The house didn't really matter, but where *was* his father, anyway?

Maybe Watson could use his Captain Conquer ring to attract Fred's attention. Watson looked at the ring, turned it around, then used the little mirror to reflect one of the big lights in the ceiling into Fred's eyes.

At first, Fred tried to brush the light away as if it were an insect. But Watson kept up his reflecting, and pretty soon Fred excused himself and walked to where Watson was standing. He grabbed Watson's hand and looked at the ring with surprise.

"Why, that's one of Sherlock Congruent's special rings. Where did you get it?"

Watson said, "I'm Sherlock Congruent's son, Watson."

"Why, of course. I thought you looked familiar. I am Fred Achziger." They shook hands gravely, just as though people were not drinking and eating and carousing all around them.

"This is a nice party," Watson said.

"Yes. When Channel Fourteen throws a retirement party, they really throw a bash. I guess they want to get rid of me pretty bad." Fred Achziger chuckled.

Watson didn't know how to react to that so he said, "My father—"

"Yes, they are putting me out to pasture. But no matter. A man with forty pounds of brains in his nose can always find something to do."

Watson said, "I heard my father and Alvin Algae talking about you. Alvin Algae said—"

This time Fred Achziger interrupted Watson by throwing back his head and laughing loudly. Then he said, "I know what Algae always says about money being more useful than brains. But I'll tell you a little secret." He leaned toward Watson and said, "I have money too." He laughed again and said, "He never did get along with anybody. It's amazing that he's such a successful agent." Suddenly, as if someone had flicked a switch, Fred Achziger became serious. "So tell me, Watson, how is your father?"

Watson waited a moment to make sure that Fred Achziger wasn't going to interrupt again. Fred Achziger waited politely, looking at Watson with an expectant expression. Watson told him about how he'd come home from school and the house and his father had been gone. He told him about the Charlieville Planning Commissioners and how they wielded a sinister power over the police. Fred Achziger nodded often.

Watson went on, "I'm sorry I'm so messy, but I had to escape through a drainpipe."

"That's all right," said Fred Achziger. "It's all in the line of duty." He looked off into space.

Watson said, "Well, so what do you think?" and ate a paper-thin slice of rare roast beef.

Without looking at Watson, Fred Achziger said, "It is obvious to me, as a man with forty pounds of brains in his nose, that someone has stolen your house and kidnapped your father. It is my opinion that these two heinous acts are connected in some way."

"I think so too," said Watson.

Fred Achziger looked at Watson strangely for a moment, as if Watson had just correctly guessed Fred Achziger's weight. He said, "Quite right. Do you know why these things have happened?"

"No."

"Of course not. You don't have forty pounds of brains in your nose. But I know. Your father was kidnapped because he was close to perfecting his motivator."

"But I thought the motivator was just pretend. Like the Great Auk and Captain Conquer and everything else on the show."

"You couldn't be more wrong. As soon as your father told me what he was building, I knew this would happen. And now it's happened. I blame myself for not insisting on protecting him."

"But why would they steal the house too?"

Fred Achziger smiled. "Where was the motivator?"

"In my dad's lab."

"And where is the lab?"

"In the back room."

"And the back room is located...?"

"In the house," Watson cried. He frowned when he thought of something else. "But who are *they* and how did *they* do it?"

"I am a man with forty pounds of brains in his nose, but even I need more information before I can tell you that. And I know just the place to get it. Let's go." He put his arm around Watson's shoulder and began to walk toward the huge elephant door.

"But wait, Mr. Achziger. All these people are here to see you. You can't leave."

"An understandable mistake, my boy. These people are not here to wish me well, though most of them do not necessarily wish me ill. They are here, just like you, for the free food and drink."

Fred Achziger waved and yelled good-bye as he hustled Watson out the door. Many people waved back and wished him good luck, but not one of them seemed inclined to leave. Watson guessed that Fred Achziger was right.

Watson walked with Fred Achziger to his car. It was an old purple Volkswagen. In the lights of the parking lot, it looked like a huge eggplant on wheels. As he got in, Watson wondered if he was doing the right thing, going off with a grown-up who claimed that he had forty pounds of brains, let alone in his nose. He remembered from biology class that the human brain weighed a couple of pounds at most.

Still, Fred Achziger was a friend of his father's and therefore not a total stranger. And though he seemed a little eccentric, wasn't that what Watson had been looking for to help him solve his mondo-bizarreo problem? He would go along with Fred Achziger for a while, until he proved himself to be totally certifiably crazy, like most of the customers of the Captain Conquer PX.

* * * * * * *

Before he started the engine, Fred Achziger took something the size of a walnut from his pocket and slipped it onto his finger. It was a Captain Conquer Signet Ring. Watson could tell, even in the dim light of the parking lot, that it was made from genuine metal-tone styrene plastic, not metal. "You never know when you will need a little help," Fred Achziger said. He backed out of his parking place at about a hundred miles an hour. Watson grabbed the handhold on the dashboard and did not let go.

The purple Volkswagen shot through the streets of Charlieville as if a madman were at the wheel. Calmly, Fred Achziger said, "I don't usually drive like this. I'm just testing your theory about the police. You'll notice that I have slid through stop signs, crept through red lights, raced beyond the speed limit, and made right turns on the red—which is also illegal in this city. No policeman has stopped us."

"Yipe!" said Watson as they went over a bump and his head almost hit the ceiling of the small car.

"Yipe, indeed," said Fred Achziger. "I am feeling pretty yipe myself, and will continue to do so till this mystery is solved. But I didn't know you spoke Clodish."

"I don't. I don't even know what Clodish is."

"Clodish is my native tongue. I haven't heard it spoken in years. *Mezzo morpho eferdent?*"

"What?"

"I was asking you in Clodish if you were enjoying the ride so far."

"It's exciting. That's for sure. But what do you think it means that we haven't been stopped by a policeman yet?"

"It means," said Fred Achziger, "that they don't want to stop us. They want us as far away from the site of the Captain Conquer PX as possible."

"Then shouldn't we go back?"

Fred Achziger put the purple Volkswagen into a tight turn, making the tires squeal against the road, swinging Watson toward him with such violence that their shoulders almost touched. They were now riding down a narrow empty road that wound between big trees. The road was dark, and Fred Achziger turned on his bright headlights.

"We will go back, all right. But not till we have

reinforcements."

"Is that where we're going now? To get reinforcements?"

"I hope so. But that remains to be seen."

Suddenly, Watson heard a siren behind them and getting closer. Out the back window he saw flashing red lights. He said, "Mr. Achziger?"

"Yes?"

"There is a policeman following us. I think he wants us to stop."

"Hmm." In the pale dashboard light Fred Achziger's face was serious. "I don't see where my theory went wrong. No matter. Perhaps after hearing what the policeman has to say I will figure it out."

The purple Volkswagen pulled over, and rolled a few feet along the bumpy shoulder. It stopped and the police car, siren no longer wailing, but still flashing its red lights, rolled to a stop behind it. One policeman walked to Fred Achziger's side of the car. The other stood ready behind the right taillight. Fred Achziger rolled down his window.

Fred Achziger had to show the policeman his driver's license, and the policeman told him that he had been driving erratically. Watson kept his hands in his pockets. He didn't want the policeman to see his ring. The policeman wrote Fred Achziger a ticket, which Watson agreed that he deserved, but then the policeman saw the ring on Fred Achziger's hand.

The policeman said, "Here's a piece of advice for you, Mr. Achziger. Stay away from the Modern Methuselah Rest Home. Do you understand? Stay away from it." The policeman sounded a little hysterical, as if what he was saying was very important, and he was afraid that Fred Achziger wouldn't understand.

"I understand," Fred Achziger said.

Both policemen got back into the car, turned around and drove back the way they'd come. Fred Achziger did not start the engine of the purple Volkswagen. The night was silent but for the singing of crickets. Watson looked at Fred Achziger. He could hear both of them breathing.

At last Fred Achziger said, "I am fortunate indeed to have forty pounds of brains in my nose. Otherwise I never would have understood what is going on."

"What is going on?" said Watson.

"You're right. Those policemen are under the sinister influence of the Planning Commission. Still, they were trying to fight the influence and help us."

"How?"

"They told us not to go to the Modern Methuselah Rest Home. When they said that, they actually meant that we must go there. We were in fact heading there when they stopped us. Perhaps that is what triggered their interest in us. This road goes nowhere else. Now I am convinced that if we are to get help, it is important that we get to the Modern Methuselah Rest Home without further delay."

He started the purple Volkswagen and they rushed off.

CHAPTER FIVE
THE MODERN
METHUSELAH REST HOME

It was a long ride to the Modern Methuselah Rest Home. The headlights of Fred Achziger's purple Volkswagen brushed across big old twisted trees and the ruins of fences as it turned this way and that following the road. "Roll down your window," Fred Achziger said, "and smell the air."

Watson did as Fred Achziger suggested, and found that the air smelled rich and green and spicy. "This is great!" Watson said. "I've never smelled anything like it in the city."

He let the air rush over him till he became too cold to stand it any longer. Then he rolled up the window and leaned back in his seat. "I'm ready for anything," he said.

"I knew the air out here in the country would have that effect on you. Now that your brain is working at its most efficient level, I will tell you about my experiences with Captain Conquer."

"Is it a long story?" Watson asked.

"Don't worry, I'll have time to finish it before we

reach the Modern Methuselah Rest Home."

Watson hadn't been worried about whether Fred Achziger would have time to finish his story. He was worried about being bored to tears. But actually, the things that Fred Achziger told Watson were pretty interesting. He had been the sound engineer on *The Adventures of Captain Conquer.*

"My biggest challenge was to find a sound the micro-brains from the Penguin Star could make when they attached themselves to their victims."

"I remember that sound," Watson said. "It was creepy."

"Thank you, Watson. We had quite a time finding a micro-brain that would make that noise. Most of them just burble, you know."

"You found micro-brains from the Penguin Star?"

"Oh, we had to special-order them, of course, through one of the big industrial supply houses that specialize in such things. I find the Catalog of Raunchypur to be the most reliable. Mostly their calls are for things like space ships, time machines, and blasters, but they have a lot of other equipment too."

"And they all work?"

"Some of them do. But most of them just make the right sound. That's all that matters."

Carefully, Watson said, "Aren't there more important things to do with a warehouse full of working space ships, time machines, and blasters than to supply sounds for TV shows?"

"Like what?" Fred Achziger wore such a look of innocent curiosity on his face that Watson decided further argument was useless. He just shrugged and said, "I don't know. There must be something."

Wasn't all this about the Catalog of Raunchypur proof enough that Fred Achziger was certifiable? Watson decided that even if Fred Achziger was crazy, he had not yet proven himself dangerous. Though the way he drove an automobile came close. Maybe Fred Achziger was lying to protect trade secrets. In any case, Watson decided that the origin of *Captain Conquer's* sound effects was not worth arguing about.

Watson said, "What will we do when we get to the Modern Methuselah Rest Home?"

"That depends a great deal on what we find when we get there. I may not know what to do. Even a man with forty pounds of brains in his nose has his limits. I only wish the Captain were here. He'd know what to do, no matter what."

Watson blurted out, "But the Captain is only a character on a TV show!" He clapped his hands over his mouth.

With sudden angry determination, Fred Achziger steered the purple Volkswagen to the side of the road and screeched to a stop. He switched off the engine with an angry flourish of his hand. The night became very quiet. Branches of trees were just a few inches away from Watson's window. They looked like witches' hands. Angrily, Fred Achziger said,

"Don't ever say that again."

"But it's true. You were the sound engineer. You must know that it's true."

"My boy, you don't have forty pounds of brains in your nose. You are young and have much to learn about life. Sometimes there is more to even a simple TV show than meets the eye. Trust me. If you do not trust me, then we must part company here."

"You mean you'd drop me here? In the middle of nowhere?"

"Everywhere is somewhere," said Fred Achziger, evading the issue. "Besides, if you don't believe in Captain Conquer, why did you go looking for his help?

Watson looked at his ring. The fact that it had already helped him out of tight spots a couple of times certainly made Captain Conquer easier to believe in.

But still, Watson had seen photographs taken during the production of *Captain Conquer* in which Webb Washington and the guy who played the bad guy stood around laughing and drinking coffee out of paper cups. Watson had met Webb Washington's agent, Alvin Algae. He knew that Captain Conquer wasn't real.

However, Watson did not want to be dropped in the middle of nowhere. He needed help to find his father and his house. So far, the only help had come from Captain Conquer, no matter how indirectly.

Even Watson could see that. Watson said, "I'm sorry I said that. I wish the Captain were here too."

"Very well, then. We'll say no more about it." Fred Achziger switched on the purple Volkswagen. The engine roared. It sounded very loud after the quiet of the countryside. Fred Achziger drove back onto the road and off into the darkness.

To see if Fred Achziger held a grudge, Watson tried to make polite conversation. He said, "We seem to be far out in the country. The Modern Methuselah Rest Home must be way outside the Charlieville city limits."

Watson was relieved when Fred Achziger answered in a calm, friendly manner: "As a matter of fact, the Modern Methuselah Rest Home lies just three feet *inside* the city limits. Tourists come from all over the world to have their pictures taken next to the sign marking the city line, with one foot in the city and one foot out. You can also buy soft drinks and postcards of jackalopes—the official animal of Charlieville—out there."

Watson had seen photographs of jackalopes, jack rabbits with horns like antelopes. He didn't believe in them any more than he believed that Fred Achziger got his sound effects from the Catalog of Raunchypur, but he didn't say anything.

After that, Watson dozed while Fred Achziger drove. Ordinarily, Watson would not have gone to bed for hours, but all the excitement and running around had made him tired. He was also a little hungry again.

Those plates at Fred Achziger's retirement party had not really been very big and Watson had not been able to go back for seconds.

It seemed that Watson had just closed his eyes when Fred Achziger shook his shoulder and said, "Wake up, Watson. We're almost there." They were just passing a big sign that said, "Modern Methuselah Rest Home— Not Just Existence, But Life!" Watson could see light through the trees. Seconds later, the purple Volkswagen swung around a bend and the Modern Methuselah Rest Home came into view at the top of a low grassy hill.

It was a big white house that reminded Watson of Scarlet O'Hara's place in *Gone With the Wind*. Thick columns out in front supported an enormous portico. Almost everyone of what seemed to be hundreds of rooms blazed with yellow light. The purple Volkswagen rolled up the long drive and rounded a wide gentle curve to park right in front of a truly impressive staircase that led up to the front door.

Fred Achziger and Watson got out of the purple Volkswagen and Watson looked in awe at the Modern Methuselah Rest Home, wondering again if anybody would notice what a mess he was. The air smelled really good out here. Fred Achziger put his arm around Watsons's shoulders and said, "Come along, my boy. Your troubles are almost over."

They walked up the stairway together. The stairs were made of wood, not marble, as Watson had guessed. When they got to the top, Fred Achziger knocked loudly on the door.

"Maybe some of the old people are sleeping," Watson said.

"Nobody goes to sleep this early," Fred Achziger said.

Still, it was a few minutes before anybody answered the door. Fred Achziger knocked again, and Watson turned to look miles across the forest through which they had just traveled. In the darkness, it looked less like a forest than a spooky, spiky fog bank.

At last, a very tall old man opened the door for them. He was thin, and wore blue jeans held up by rainbow suspenders. Fred Achziger was about to speak when the man held a thick-jointed finger to his lips, said "Shush!" and motioned them to enter. Surprisingly, Fred Achziger actually did not speak, but nodded at Watson and followed the old man.

The entire inside of the house looked as if it had been carved out of a single piece of dark wood. And though Watson could not identify the odor that filled the place, it was thick and warm—full of onions and spices—and smelled wonderful, like a restaurant that specialized in the food of some country he'd never heard of.

There was no way to walk softly across the squeaky old hardwood floor, past the wide stairway that rose to the second floor, and through a double doorway to a big brightly lit room filled with old people. Around the double doorway were small windows with geometric patterns sandblasted into them. Paintings of gardens and a blue man playing a blue guitar were hung on the green flowered wallpaper.

The old people were dressed casually, but they were all neat and clean. Three couples wearing earphones connected to tiny radios hooked to their belts danced to what was obviously a bouncy tune. A few old people sat on a long couch reading thick leather-bound books.

In the center of the room, a card table with three men and a woman seated around it had attracted a lot of attention. The four players were concentrating hard on the cards in their hands. In the center of the table two dice lay on a game board.

One of the men was very tall—even sitting down. He wore a long robe with wide vertical stripes. He had curly white hair that frothed over the top of his head and down his face to make a biblical beard.

Across from him sat an old man without any hair on his head at all. He was not fat, or even chubby, but solidly built, like a hunk of cheese. He had intense black eyes, and a nose that pointed down as if it were trying to meet his upturned chin. He was wearing a light cotton shirt, a blue cardigan sweater, and wide brown pants. Watson knew him from somewhere, but he did not know where that place was.

The third man had distinguished white hair and

kept twirling the tips of his thin white mustache.

The woman looked plump and sweet. She pushed her tiny gold-rimmed glasses up on her nose and threw a card onto the table. She said, "Take that, Destructowitz!" She leaned back in her chair with her arms folded and glowered triumphantly at the other three. The crowd of old people observing mumbled to themselves.

"Excuse me," said Fred Achziger.

The audience looked at Fred Achziger and Watson. The thin old man with the suspenders held his finger to his lips again. Fred Achziger sighed and folded his arms.

The three men looked at the cards in their hands and at each other. Then as one, they threw their cards onto the table. "We give up, Mazie," the bald man said. His voice was as familiar to Watson as his face. Who was this guy?

While the rest of the crowd congratulated Mazie, Fred Achziger put his hand on the bald man's shoulder. "Martin?"

The man twisted in his chair to look at Fred Achziger. He grinned and leaped to his feet and grabbed Fred Achziger's hand and began to pump it as if he thought it might give water if he pumped hard enough. "Fred! Fred Achziger! Why, I haven't seen you in years!" He looked at Watson and said, "And who is this?"

"This is Watson Congruent. You know, Sherlock Congruent's boy."

"Of course! Sherlock has spoken of you often!" He dropped Fred Achziger's hand and began to pump Watson's.

"Do I know you?" asked Watson.

The bald man stopped pumping Watson's hand and stood back beaming, his hands on his hips. Fred Achziger said, "Watson, I want to introduce Martin Trent."

"How d'you do? I'm sure I know you from somewhere," Watson said.

"You ever watch *The Adventures of Captain Conquer*?"

"Sure. My father and I watch—well, we used to watch it all the time."

"This," said Fred Achziger as proudly as if he'd invented him, "is Martin Trent, the man who played Captain Conquer's sidekick, Chuckles."

"Of course, I had more hair back then." Martin Trent used one hand to brush back imaginary hair on his bald head. He and Watson shook hands again, Watson with more enthusiasm this time.

Martin Trent said, "What brings you out this way, Fred?"

"The young man here has a little problem. I thought you might be able to help."

"I'm a lot older than I was when I fought crime with the Captain."

Fred Achziger said, "At least hear him out. Is there someplace we can talk?"

"Right here," Martin Trent said, and sat back

down at the card table. The other three chairs were now empty; Fred Achziger and Watson each took one. Like conspirators, they leaned together over the table and with Fred Achziger's help, Watson told Martin Trent about the disappearance of his father and their house. No one else in the room seemed to be paying any attention to them.

When Watson finished his story, Martin Trent made funny motions with his mouth, pulling his lips over one way and then over the other. Watson could tell he was thinking. Martin Trent shook his head. "Like I say, Fred, it's been a long time since I fought crime with the Captain."

"You always did like to be coaxed," said Fred Achziger. To Watson he said, "Show him the ring."

Watson pulled his hand from his pocket and held out his metal Captain Conquer Signet Ring.

"Great Frooth," Martin Trent said. "That looks like one of those rings from the Catalog of Raunchypur!"

Fred Achziger said, "Perhaps it is even more authentic than that."

Watson noticed that the couples had stopped dancing and that the people on the couch had stopped reading. They, and all the folks who had been watching the game at the card table, were gathered around again, staring at Watson's ring.

"This is serious, then," said Martin Trent.

"I, a man with forty pounds of brains in his nose, suspect that alien beings may be involved."

Martin Trent nodded. He raised his voice and looked around. "Well then," he said. "Shall we help the lad?"

The old people cheered and shook their arms in the air. They slapped Watson on the back. He couldn't help smiling. He shouted to be heard over the cheering, "Why are all these people suddenly so interested in helping me?"

Martin Trent held up his hands and the cheering gradually stopped. He said, "I've made everyone in the Modern Methuselah Rest Home a member of the Captain's loyal legion of followers, the Conquer Corps. We'd like to fight crime and injustice all the time, but most of us don't have the energy we used to. We've been biding our time, honing our skills by playing the Captain Conquer game." He tapped the game board they had been leaning on. Watson saw that it featured a likeness of Webb Washington and the words OFFICIAL CAPTAIN CONQUER GAME. "We've been waiting for a crime worthy of us and of Captain Conquer. This is it!"

Everybody cheered again.

* * * * * *

Watson was delighted to discover his father had been right about Captain Conquer fans being one big happy family, but he was not confident about their abilities. After all, how much could playing a board game prepare a person for fighting a real criminal? And these people were old. Really old.

The youngest of them was at least as old as Fred Achziger, and most of them were older.

Still, a lot of strange things had happened that day. He might do worse than giving Martin Trent's Conquer Corps a chance.

"What's our next move?" Martin Trent said. Fred Achziger tapped the Captain Conquer game board but didn't say anything.

Watson said, "I know." Fred Achziger looked at him with raised eyebrows.

Watson pulled a rather crumpled and dirty sheet of paper from his pocket. He smoothed it out on the table.

Fred Achziger picked it up and looked at it. "Why, this is just some kind of notice from the Charlieville Planning Commission. A clue?"

"Look at the other side," said Martin Trent, who was looking at the other side. "It's not only a clue. It's in code!"

Fred Achziger turned the paper over and squinted at the code. "Of course. We must decode it immediately."

"I haven't had a chance to figure it out yet," said Watson.

"Then we'll do it right now," said Fred Achziger. "Please give me your ring." Watson put his ring into Fred Achziger's extended hand. "Read me the letters, Martin, and I'll decode them for you."

Watson watched while Martin wrote down the letters that Fred Achziger decoded by spinning the pointer on the Captain Conquer ring. Soon, the message looked like this:

Bring Berkowitz to Captain Conquer's lab
zpgle zcpimugrx rm aynrygl amloscpq jyz

"But what does it mean?" said Watson. "And who is Berkowitz?"

"Ah," said Fred Achziger. "Even Martin knows Berkowitz. As for what the message means, I'm not surprised you don't understand it. You haven't got forty pounds of brains in your nose."

Martin Trent said, "Clifford Berkowitz used to build the props for the Captain Conquer show."

"The man was a genius. Perhaps he still is. We must find him and take him to the Captain's laboratory."

"That's what it says, all right," Watson said, "but what does it mean?" He chose his next words carefully, not wanting to upset anybody. "I didn't know the Captain had a laboratory outside the TV show."

Fred Achziger and Martin Trent looked mysteriously at each other. "He didn't," Fred Achziger said. "The TV show laboratory will do quite well enough."

Martin Trent said, "The question remains: Who wants Berkowitz, and why?"

Watson said, "I don't know. I found the message with the ring in the empty lot where my house used to be."

Fred Achziger said, "I see, then, that we don't really know where this message comes from. It may be leading us into a trap."

"The Captain used to walk into traps on purpose sometimes because that was the only way to learn more about the criminals he was fighting."

"If this is a trap," said Watson, "we may have trouble escaping from it."

"The Captain always found a way," Martin Trent said simply.

"It's decided, then," said Fred Achziger. "As a man with forty pounds of brains in his nose I suggest we find Clifford Berkowitz, take him to the laboratory, and see what happens."

That didn't sound like much of a plan to Watson, but he didn't have a better one.

Martin Trent told them that the last he had heard from Berkowitz, he lived far out in the country, and they would run out of road long before they got there. Fred Achziger said, "We'll need flashlights and a compass."

"Right here in my ring," said Watson.

"Very well," said Fred Achziger. "We leave tonight."

CHAPTER SIX
GOPHER BROKE

"But first," said Fred Achziger, "I suggest we prepare ourselves for the ordeal to come by dining on some of Methuselah's fine food. I don't know when we'll eat again."

"I already had dinner," said Martin Trent, "but you two go ahead."

"Ordeal?" said Watson.

"Just a figure of speech," said Fred Achziger. Martin Trent winked at Watson and said, "He hopes. I'll tell Methuselah to bring out the leftovers," He quickly walked out a side door.

The old people went back to what they had been doing before, dancing or reading or whatever, but occasionally one of them would walk by the table and smile and nod.

Fred Achziger said, "Would you care to play a round of the Official Captain Conquer Game while we're waiting?"

Watson shrugged. "Sure. It'll toughen us up for the ordeal to come."

Without smiling, Fred Achziger said, "Even a

man with forty pounds of brains in his nose can use a little combat training." Fred Achziger was entirely serious as he squared up the deck of cards and shuffled them. Watson crossed his arms and tried to be as serious as Fred Achziger.

But Fred Achziger had barely begun to explain the rules when the big froth-haired man in the striped robe marched in through the door that Martin Trent had just gone out of. He was carrying a tray that was about the same size as the one Watson had carried to get into Fred Achziger's retirement party. The appetizing warm odor that permeated the Modern Methuselah Rest Home became so strong that Watson felt he could eat the odor itself and never be hungry again.

Fred Achziger and Watson pushed the Captain Conquer game aside. Smiling broadly, Methuselah put down the tray. He stood back and clasped his hands and said, "Eat! Eat! Look at you, how skinny!"

Watson had never seen food like this before. At home, his father normally cooked out of frozen boxes or freeze-dried bags or cans. On the rare occasions when they could afford to eat at a restaurant, they had hamburgers at a chain. It was OK food, but nothing special.

The food on the tray had a heaviness, a solidity, a reality, that Watson had never before seen in food. There were piles of potatoes, both mashed and whole, gobs of noodles with raisins and spices in them, light brown things that looked like small delicate burritos but smelled like sweet cheese, stacks of corn on the cob, sliced meat that steamed a heavenly succulent fragrance. The whole production looked and smelled so good that Watson almost cried for joy because all of his life, it was this stuff on this platter that he'd wanted to eat, only he hadn't known it till now.

Fred Achziger dug in immediately, taking great serving spoons full of food onto his plate. Watson must have lingered too long appreciating the layout because Methuselah wailed, "He doesn't like it!" then took up a spoon and a plate and began to serve Watson himself, saying, "Here, try some of this. I'm sure you'll like that. Just a little of this other thing would be good...."

Everything had onions and spices and vegetables he didn't recognize mixed in with it. Watson never before had eaten so much at one sitting. He washed it all down with a kind of soda pop that Methuselah called "two cents plain." It was nothing but water and fizz, and Methuselah served it by squeezing the lever on a big glass bottle and allowing the sparkling water to gush into a glass.

When they were done, Watson and Fred Achziger were happy and filled to bursting. Martin Trent, now wearing a long brown coat, suggested that they could rest in the car on the way to Berkowitz's house. The two men and the boy rushed out of the room just as Methuselah appeared at the kitchen door with another big tray and yelled after them, "What about dessert?"

* * * * * * *

It was cold outside after the warmth of the Modern Methuselah Rest Home. The three bundled into the purple Volkswagen. Fred Achziger drove, Martin Trent sat in front next to him, and Watson sat in back, looking out between the front seats.

Fred Achziger steered the purple Volkswagen along the same road they had taken from the center of the city. Not far from the Modern Methuselah Rest Home Watson saw a big sign with a neon arrow and a running neon jackalope. The sign said, "Gas Food—See the Charlieville City Line—Gas Food." It was gone in an instant, flung back in the darkness.

Pretty soon the road began to climb ever more steeply into the forest. While Fred Achziger and Martin Trent talked over old times in low voices, Watson fell against the back seat and slept.

He awoke with a snort when the motion of the car changed. They were bouncing around in their seats despite the fact that the car was slowing down. "Where are we?" Watson said as he sat up, rubbing his eyes. Fred Achziger drove slowly and carefully, and still they bounced around as the car rolled into potholes and over bumps.

"Two or three miles from where Berkowitz lives, is my guess," said Martin Trent.

"Quite right," said Fred Achziger. "And I think that we will have to walk."

Indeed, the forest was closing in on the climbing lumpy road, and soon it was not possible for the purple Volkswagen to navigate between the trees. When Fred Achziger turned off the engine, the car rolled back into a pothole and stopped. They looked around them.

In the headlights, the view up the slope was fascinating, but it did not promise a pleasant walk. All around them big trees with smooth bark were tangled in brush below and in slim vines above. Leaves stirred in the wind and gave Watson the impression that big toothy animals were waiting for them to leave the car. Three men in a can— what a treat for some beast!

"Are you sure about this?" Watson said.

"I have forty pounds of brains in my nose."

Watson could see that that settled the matter for Fred Achziger. He opened the car door and got out, but stood within the shelter of the door as if it were a shield.

Martin Trent said, "I haven't been out here for years, and that one time Berkowitz guided me. But this looks right. He's kind of a hermit." He got out and left the door open. Watson quickly followed and stood behind him looking around. The air was cold, and it still smelled good, but the forest itself looked sinister because it was so wild and dark.

The three of them stood near the car listening to

a gentle night wind sigh through the trees. Watson shivered. Fred Achziger reached in and turned off the headlights. Immediately the darkness jumped at them as if it were an animal. For a second, Watson was frightened and didn't know what to do. "Your ring," Fred Achziger said. Watson switched on his Captain Conquer emergency light. Now the forest looked artificial, and its shadows wavered as Watson moved. He said, "Which way?"

"From here?" Martin Trent said. "East, I would say."

"Unfortunately, you are correct," Fred Achziger said.

Watson led the way uphill into the forest primeval. Fred Achziger came next, doing his best with the glowing plastic pimple and snip of tin compass on his genuine metal-tone styrene plastic Captain Conquer ring. He and Martin Trent stayed well within the circle of light cast by Watson's ring. They crunched through the underbrush as they climbed.

"Careful of poison ivy," said Fred Achziger.

"And worse," said Martin Trent.

Fred Achziger mumbled as they walked.

"What?" asked Watson as he brushed a low branch out of his way.

"I'm counting steps," Fred Achziger said. "Ninety- eight, ninety-nine, one hundred, hundred-one...."

He sounded breathless to Watson. As a matter of

fact, all three of them were breathing pretty hard, making noises like old machinery. Watson had never walked through a forest at night, especially uphill, and he doubted if either Fred Achziger or Martin Trent had either.

Suddenly something leaped onto Watson's shoulder. He jumped and looked around. The thing on his shoulder was Fred Achziger's hand. Fred Achziger lifted it off and said, "I have counted one hundred fifty steps. We must now turn at right angles and walk due north."

"Next time," Watson said, "please warn me when you are trying to get my attention."

Marlin Trent looked around them and said, "Was it one hundred fifty? I thought it was one hundred seventy-five."

Fred Achziger looked at him severely. "One hundred fifty. Must I remind you—"

"Never argue with a man who has forty pounds of brains in his nose," Watson finished for him. He turned, and using his Captain Conquer compass, walked due north. Fred Achziger and Martin Trent followed. It was unpleasant to walk with one foot upslope and the other foot downslope. All three bobbed as they walked.

They walked through a thicket of prickly branches. It felt to Watson as if the forest were trying to hold him back, prevent him from finding Berkowitz and then his father.

Just that afternoon, Watson had been in school.

So much had happened since that it seemed as if all his former life had occurred years ago. He had always been tramping through this forest. Always would. He called out, "How much farther do we walk in this direction?"

"Till we get to the dead tree with the noose," said Fred Achziger.

"Noose?" said Watson.

"Don't worry about it," said Fred Achziger as they continued to tramp along. "Berkowitz hung it there himself."

"As a warning?" Watson said.

"No," said Martin Trent. "He has a flair for the dramatic."

Watson nodded. Sure. Why not? He was walking now without thinking much about anything but how cold he was and their next landmark, the dead tree with the noose. Merely walking was an end in itself, putting one foot in front of another, avoiding uneven ground where he could trip or turn an ankle, ducking under branches. He became aware that for some time he'd been hearing the sound of someone following them.

"Stop," he whispered hoarsely, and held up his hand the way pioneer guides in the movies did. Fred Achziger and Martin Trent gathered around him. "What is it?" Fred Achziger said.

"Listen," said Watson.

All three struck attitudes of listening. Martin Trent put his hand to his ear; Fred Achziger held his nose into the air the way a dog might; Watson stood without moving a muscle. There it was again, a crackling of sticks breaking underfoot, the rustle of leaves and—yes—a sound like that of a crazy person laughing softly to himself.

Fred Achziger lowered his nose and said, "Oh that! Nothing to worry about."

"But what is it?" said Martin Trent.

"Animals, of course. But they're not dangerous."

"How do you know?" said Watson.

Fred Achziger tapped the side of his nose. "If they eat you, I'll take full responsibility. Let's continue."

To Watson's frozen brain, continuing sounded like a good idea. He would be warmer moving than he was standing still. If the animals were all around them, and they seemed to be, going back might be just as dangerous as going forward. He stepped off again, pushing the darkness away with the emergency light of his Captain Conquer ring.

Eventually, they came to the dead tree with the noose hanging from it.

Perhaps Berkowitz *had* tied the noose there. If so, his dramatic flair had paid off. It was a grim sight, hanging from a dried-out husk of a tree that still raised empty branches to the sky as if pleading for mercy.

They sat down with their backs to the tree, breathing hard. "Is it much farther?" said Watson.

"Not much," said Fred Achziger. "We go east again, now." He stood up and looked expectantly at Watson. Watson checked his Captain Conquer compass and trudged up the mountain.

Watson had not walked more than ten paces when he came to a clearing. His light did not go very far, but he could tell from the wind in the trees and the way the sounds of his own movement were whirled away by the wind that the clearing was huge. The ground he could see in his umbrella of light was punctured every few feet with small round holes, each with its little mound of dirt. The head of a fur-faced animal suddenly popped up from one of the holes. It twitched its whiskers at them and watched with some interest as they passed.

"Gophers," said Martin Trent.

"Yes," said Fred Achziger. "As I recall, Berkowitz keeps them as pets. I'm sure it was they who were following us."

After walking up the mountain through the forest, Watson was even dirtier than he had been before. But he didn't feel so bad about it because Fred Achziger and Martin Trent were also spattered with mud and had leaves in their hair. (Martin Trent didn't actually have leaves in his hair, of course, but one big brown one was plastered to his bald pate, looking as if it had been painted on.)

Watson approached a small building that stood on a level place. A faded and warped sign over it said TICKETS, and featured the picture of some animal. The sign was too faded to tell what the animal was. It could have been a gopher.

"Wait," said Fred Achziger. Watson stopped. Fred Achziger called out, "Berkowitz? Are you in there?"

A voice came from inside the ticket booth. "Who wants to know?"

"Friends."

"Wonderful. When I need friends, I'll call you."

"It's me, Berkowitz, Martin Trent. I have Fred Achziger and Sherlock Congruent's son, Watson, with me."

After a short pause, the man inside the ticket booth called out, "The son of Sherlock Congruent? Why didn't you say so? Come ahead."

They walked forward and had to step over a gopher that was sleeping in front of the door. The door creaked open. Watson, Fred Achziger, and Martin Trent crowded themselves into one end of the booth.

Most of the room was taken up by a fat old man wearing gray pants and a lumberjack shirt. He was rocking in a big shiny rocking chair, holding a gopher that was curled up in his lap like a cat. He was scratching it behind the ears. On his head the man wore a headdress made of wire hangers and scrunched-up aluminum foil.

On the wall behind him was a big sign that said SEE PENGUINLAND and then a schedule of entrance fees. Watson decided that the animal on the TICKETS sign was probably a penguin. The room was almost as cold as the forest itself, though it seemed warmer because the walls of the room cut the wind.

The man in the rocking chair pretended not to notice them, though ignoring another person would have been almost impossible in the tiny room. Suddenly Berkowitz looked up as if he were surprised to see them. Then he smiled so that his eyes crinkled up and almost disappeared. He said, "The gophers told me that people were coming, but I wasn't told how important my visitors would be."

"It's good to see you again, Berkowitz," said Martin Trent.

"Is that you, Chuckles?" said Berkowitz. "My, but time has played hob with your scalp. And can that be you, Fred? Do you still have thirty-five pounds of brains in your nose?"

"Forty now," said Fred Achziger proudly.

"You live in this place?" said Watson.

"That must be Sherlock Congruent's boy, Watson. Impolite little whelp, isn't he?" Berkowitz laughed.

"Apologize to Mr. Berkowitz," said Fred Achziger.

"Not necessary," said Berkowitz. "He'd be blind if he wasn't curious. No, I don't live up here. This is just my lookout post. The gophers have dug me a warm dry apartment below." He pointed at the ground with one thumb. He chuckled again, stopped abruptly and said, "But tell me what brings you three out here. It can't be a social call."

"It isn't," said Martin Trent.

"Tell him, Watson," said Fred Achziger.

For the third time that evening, Watson told about how he had come home from school to find both his father and his house gone, only a metal Captain Conquer ring left behind.

"Let me see the ring," Berkowitz said.

When Watson showed it to him, Berkowitz almost pulled off Watson's finger, trying to look at it. "That ring was obviously made by the same aliens I've been communicating with for years."

"Aliens?" said Watson.

"Aliens, indeed. Aliens. But before I tell you about them, you tell me why you're here. It can't be just to show me that ring."

"No," said Fred Achziger. "There was a coded message with the ring. It asked that we take you to the Captain's laboratory."

"Hah!" said Berkowitz. "Let me see the message." Watson pulled the paper from his pocket and handed it to him. Berkowitz rubbed it between thumb and forefinger while he studied it carefully. He handed it back to Watson and said, "I see. This has the fine hand of the Puddentakers in it."

"Puddentakers?" said the other three all at once.

"Yes. The aliens I was telling you about. Everything I built for *Captain Conquer* was designed from patterns I purchased from the Catalog of Raunchypur."

"You mean you've been dealing for years with the same aliens who kidnapped my father?" Watson was astonished.

"They didn't kidnap anybody back in the old days," Berkowitz said.

Fred Achziger nodded gravely and said, "Policies on Puddentake must have changed radically."

Berkowitz said, "I guess that's why I haven't been getting my new Raunchypur catalogs lately."

"Uh," said Watson innocently, "do you have a copy of your latest catalog? I've heard a lot about those catalogs and I'd sure like to see one."

"Not in much of a hurry to save your father, are you, Watson?" said Berkowitz.

"If the Catalog of Raunchypur has something to do with the aliens who have my father, I want to have a look at it. It may be important."

"Bravo," said Fred Achziger. "I was about to ask to see the catalog myself. It's been a long time, and a new issue comes out every year."

Berkowitz chuckled. He said, "All right, then. You three wait here." He stood up, spilling the gopher from his lap the way he might have unloaded a cat, and tilted the rocking chair sideways. A trap-door attached to the bottom of the chair opened, allowing bright orange light to escape from below. Watson could hear the chittering of hundreds of gophers. Their smell rose too, like that of acres of wet carpet. "I'll be right back," said Berkowitz as he descended, the orange light illuminating his face and making the contraption on his head look like gold.

When he was gone, Watson said, "Kind of eccentric, isn't he?"

"He is a genius," said Fred Achziger.

"I've never seen so many gophers," said Martin Trent.

Fred Achziger said, "The word gopher comes from either the French word for the verb to tunnel, or the French word for honeycomb." He tapped the side of his nose.

After a good deal of banging around below, Berkowitz returned with a big book under his arm and a cigar box in one hand. Whatever was in the cigar box was rolling around, making a lot of noise. Berkowitz tilted the rocking chair back onto the floor, and settled into it. He set the cigar box on the floor and handed the book to Watson.

Watson studied the Catalog of Raunchypur in the light of his Captain Conquer ring. He turned page after page, becoming more confused as he went on. It didn't make any sense. At last he handed the catalog to Fred Achziger, who began to thumb through it greedily. Watson said, "I don't understand. That looks just like an April Limited mail order catalog."

"Well, of course it does," said Berkowitz. "It's in code. We wouldn't want just anybody to know what's in this catalog."

"What do you mean?" said Watson.

"It's simple." Berkowitz deftly pulled the Catalog of Raunchypur from Fred Achziger's hands, and held it open to a page for Watson. "What do you see on this page?" he said.

"Underwear," said Watson.

"Underwear is code for space suits," said Berkowitz.

"It's true," said Fred Achziger. "And barbecue tools is code for blasters and tents is code for space ships."

"This is all pretty strange," said Watson.

"Ingenious," said Martin Trent.

"And the Catalog of Raunchypur just sent you this stuff through the mail?" said Watson.

Berkowitz said, "Only the pieces in greatest demand. They came from the Puddentakers' Raunchypur warehouse right here in Charlieville." He riffled the pages of the catalog with his thumb. "The Puddentakers sent plans for the more unusual equipment through the sub-ether. I used to receive the information over my sub-ether antenna." He touched his hat of scrunched-up aluminum foil and wire hangers.

"Did you have a hat like this too?" Watson asked Fred Achziger.

"Nope. Didn't need it in the old days. Neither did Berkowitz. Postal regulations were less strict about sending Raunchypur information or merchandise through the mail."

Berkowitz said, "This sub-ether antenna also allows me to talk to animals. That's how I manage with the gophers."

"And they understand you?" said Watson.

"Better than some people."

Watson didn't think that was much of an answer. He could see how any normal person would have trouble understanding Berkowitz.

Berkowitz said, "Look here. Puddentaker relics," and showed him the contents of his cigar box. The box was full of small stones, old spark plugs, empty sardine tins, and coffee-tin lids.

Watson said, "Hmm." Then he picked up a shard of pottery that had a four-armed man with the head of a bird painted on it. Part of his right leg was missing. The box also contained a small piece of machined metal. It looked like a three-dimensional maze. The metal felt greasy, though no grease was on it, and touching it made Watson's hand tingle.

"Pretty convincing, eh?" said Martin Trent.

"Convincing enough, I suppose," said Watson. "Will you come with us to the Captain's laboratory?"

Berkowitz grabbed the cigar box away from Watson and said, "I will not."

"But why?" Watson said.

"Because I can see from that ring you are wearing that the people who kidnapped your father and your house are aliens from Puddentake. The only reason they could have for kidnapping him is that they want him to work on their Captain Conquer equipment. They are very big Captain Conquer fans."

"But the Captain Conquer equipment originally came from them," said Watson. "How could my father know more about it than the Puddentakers?"

Fred Achziger said, "Not all Captain Conquer equipment, Watson. Just motivators. Remember, he was working on one when he was kidnapped. His researches must have taken him far beyond the knowledge of even the Puddentakers themselves. Perhaps even into the realm of super-motivators."

"Your dad's a smart fellow," said Martin Trent.

"But that doesn't explain why Mr. Berkowitz won't come with us."

"That much is obvious," said Fred Achziger. "Our friend Berkowitz is angry that your father was kidnapped instead of him."

"I know more about the Captain's equipment than anybody. The Puddentakers ought to know that."

"You're sure it's motivators they want?" said Watson.

"Undoubtedly," said Fred Achziger.

Watson cried out, "But my father had no control over being kidnapped. If it had been up to him, I'm sure he would have sent the Puddentakers to you."

Berkowitz crossed his arms and looked up into a corner of the room. "That's easy to say now," he said.

It was quiet in the ticket booth. Watson listened to the wind and the small scratchings of the gophers. What were he and Fred Achziger and Martin Trent waiting for? They had a long walk back to the car ahead of them, and it wasn't getting any earlier.

Fred Achziger laid a finger aside his nose and said, "Perhaps our friend Berkowitz would agree to this: Perhaps he will return with us to the Modern Methuselah Rest Home and wait there with the residents while we visit the laboratory. He can lead the reinforcements, should that become necessary."

Berkowitz didn't move. He still stared at the corner of the ceiling.

"Come, come," said Fred Achziger. "The boy is in trouble. He is the son of Sherlock Congruent. You owe him that much."

Still without moving, Berkowitz said, "Very well. I haven't seen my old friend Methuselah for years. Is his food as good as ever?"

"Better," said Martin Trent.

"I'll get my coat," said Berkowitz.

CHAPTER SEVEN
DOWN IN THE LABORATORY

It took forever for Berkowitz to get ready to leave. Watson, Fred Achziger, and Martin Trent stood around in various attitudes of boredom while Berkowitz banged and thumped and slid things around in his underground apartment.

Berkowitz also kept up a running commentary to himself. He said, "Oh yes, sure I'll help. Of course. Just because you want Sherlock Congruent instead of me. Oho! Just step right up and insult the old man. Sure! Of course!" And so on. He was really steamed that the Puddentakers had kidnapped Watson's father instead of him.

Watson said to Martin Trent, "It sure would have saved me a lot of trouble if the Puddentakers had kidnapped Berkowitz instead of my father."

"Maybe next time," said Martin Trent. He smiled sympathetically and patted Watson's hand.

After a while Berkowitz came upstairs. He was still wearing his sub-ether antenna. Watson thought he was ready to go after he lowered his rocking chair back over the secret trapdoor, but Berkowitz insisted on saying good-bye to each of his gophers individually. Gophers were everywhere. Watson leaned against the wall of the ticket booth, hugging himself to keep warm and watched Berkowitz rub noses with his pets.

His leave-taking did not seem to make much of an impression on the gophers, but saying good-bye evidently was a strong emotional experience for Berkowitz. He sniffled a lot and he seemed close to tears.

"I haven't been parted from them for ten years," Berkowitz said, sobbing.

He waved to the gophers from the edge of the open field around the ticket booth, and cried, "Goodbye! Good-bye! I'll be back soon," even while Fred Achziger and Martin Trent dragged him into the forest.

The group walked back down to the tree with the noose, and Fred Achziger began to walk south across the mountain, but Berkowitz said, "No. This way." His eyes were still red, but his voice was steady.

"We're going back to the road," Martin Trent said.

"I know where you're going. Follow me." He set off down the hill in a direction which, according to Watson's ring, was sort of southwest.

Watson, Fred Achziger, and Martin Trent looked at each other, shrugged, and followed. They walked together in the light cast by Watson's ring, but

Berkowitz didn't seem to need it. He just plunged into the forest, sensing his way by sound and smell and feel. Any way but sight, because outside the umbrella of Watson's light, it was too dark to see anything but the occasional glimmer of shine off a smooth leaf or the trunk of a tree.

After they'd walked for a while, Fred Achziger called a halt and sat down on a fallen tree. "As a man with forty pounds of brains in his nose, I say we're lost."

Berkowitz stopped and turned to glare at him. Watson and Martin Trent stood near Fred Achziger, but did not sit on the tree. Berkowitz said, "Those are city brains. They're no good here. I know this forest. We're almost there." Without waiting for an answer, Berkowitz turned, forced his way through a curtain of tall weeds, and disappeared into the undergrowth. Watson could still hear him marching ahead, but the sound was fading.

"We'll be lost for sure," said Watson, "if we don't follow him." He walked after Berkowitz.

"Come on, Fred. A man with forty pounds of brains in his nose ought to be able to accept help when he needs it," said Martin Trent. He walked after Watson. Watson looked back and saw Fred Achziger rising unhappily from his fallen tree and following Martin Trent.

They caught up with Berkowitz, who looked back at them and grumbled, "Hah! Lost, am I?" He turned and with renewed energy began to walk again. Watson could still hear him muttering, "Imagine! A man who knows so much about Captain Conquer and the Puddentakers, pressed into service as a native guide...." He went on in a voice so low that Watson could not understand him.

Fred Achziger said, "Someday, Berkowitz will appreciate the resource embodied in a man who has forty pounds of brains in his nose." He was breathing hard, making that old machine noise again.

"Absolutely," said Martin Trent.

Moments later, they arrived at the road. The wind washed leaves across it in tiny whirlwinds. It was full of holes, dips, and bumps. Watson could see why the ride had been so bumpy on their arrival. Berkowitz was waiting for them with his arms folded. "Lost, huh?" he said.

Watson and the others looked around. Fred Achziger said, "As a man with forty pounds of brains in his nose, I have a question for the man who isn't lost. Where is the car?"

"You worry too much. Come on." Berkowitz walked off as hard as he could go.

"As a man with—"

Martin Trent interrupted Fred Achziger by saying, "I know how many pounds of brains you have in your nose, but I think maybe Berkowitz knows what he's doing." He followed Berkowitz.

Watson put his hand on Fred Achziger's arm. The purple suit was covered with wrinkles and blotches of dirt. Neither Martin Trent nor Watson was any cleaner. Fred Achziger's retirement party had happened a long time ago. Even the Modern Methuselah Rest Home seemed to have been located in another world.

"Come on," said Watson. "We've all been through a lot today. I'm sure your forty pounds of brains will work again once we get back to the city."

"You think so?" Fred Achziger said.

"Sure. Come on." They hurried after Berkowitz and Martin Trent.

The road became a rutted path after a while, and soon Watson could see the taillights of the purple Volkswagen reflected in the light from his Captain Conquer ring. Berkowitz and Martin Trent were talking in low voices while they waited.

Though Berkowitz was rocking up and back on his heels and smiling, Fred Achziger said nothing to him. He walked straight to the car, got in, and started the engine. Martin Trent and Watson climbed into the back seat. Berkowitz got into the front next to Fred Achziger. No one said a word.

Fred Achziger allowed the purple Volkswagen to roll backwards down the mountain until it came to a place that was wide enough to allow him to turn around. Soon, they were riding over the bumpy road back toward Charlieville.

* * * * * * *

As the road became less rumpled, and the passengers stopped bouncing around inside the purple Volkswagen, all four of them relaxed. Berkowitz said, "Tell me about the last meal you had at the Modern Methuselah Rest Home."

"Last meal?" said Martin Trent. His voice squeaked.

"You know what he means," said Fred Achziger. "This is no time for comedy relief."

"Sorry," said Martin Trent. "Old habits die hard."

Fred Achziger told Berkowitz about the dinner in some detail, calling the items on the menu by names that Watson had never heard before and that slipped away from his memory a moment after he'd heard them. Berkowitz's eyes got bigger and bigger, and he made a funny wet smacking sound with his lips as he worked his mouth. When Fred Achziger was done, Berkowitz said, "I've been eating roots and berries for almost ten years. Have you any idea how boring roots and berries get to be?"

"What about birds and rabbits?" Watson said.

"I'm not Davy Crockett, young man. I'm as much a city boy as ol' Fred here. The birds and rabbits are few and far between."

"Why not just live in the city?"

"I'm a hermit, boy. Hermits don't live in cities. If they did, they wouldn't be hermits. Got it?" He watched the forest passing outside his window. "You can't fight what you are. Someday you'll learn that."

Watson decided that if he turned out to be something like a hermit when he grew up, he'd fight it like mad.

"Boy, it'll be good to eat Methuselah's food," said Berkowitz. "You say he has blintzes?"

Fred Achziger assured Berkowitz that he did.

Berkowitz made that wet sound with his mouth again. Watson guessed that Berkowitz looked forward to Methuselah's food the way a drowning man looks forward to oxygen.

When they passed the big neon sign at the Charlieville city limits, Berkowitz said, "I visited this place when I was no older than you, Watson." Berkowitz sounded sad. "Ah, those were the days. You know, before I kept gophers, I kept jackalopes."

"Is that so?" said Watson. This seemed unlikely to him.

"I know they're kind of rare, but I had a whole herd of them. Here. Look." Berkowitz pulled his wallet from somewhere among his rumpled clothes and took out a folded piece of cardboard. He handed it to Watson. It was an old brown photograph of Berkowitz nearly buried in a heap of rabbity animals that had horns like antelopes. The picture didn't look faked to Watson.

Martin Trent leaned over to look and said, "Gee, I remember when I took that picture."

"There was a time," Fred Achziger said, "when jackalopes roamed the plains like the buffalo. You could wait all day while one herd passed."

Watson handed the picture back to Berkowitz, determined to check out this jackalope stuff in his encyclopedia when he found his house. "Hmm. Interesting," he said.

Lights were still on when the purple Volkswagen pulled up in front of the Modern Methuselah Rest Home. Music was playing too. It was a bouncy tune that made Watson tap his toes. Berkowitz wished them good luck looking for Watson's father.

Fred Achziger said, "A man with forty pounds of brains in his nose doesn't need luck. We'll find Sherlock Congruent. You be ready with the reinforcements."

"You worry too much," said Berkowitz. He slammed the car door and ran up the steps to the Modern Methuselah Rest Home.

As they drove off, Watson said, "Can we trust him?"

"We may argue, but Berkowitz and I are like brothers," said Fred Achziger. "You can trust him as you would trust me."

Watson nodded and hoped for the best.

Fred Achziger drove more carefully than he had when he and Watson had driven out of Charlieville. He didn't want the police stopping them now, especially knowing that the police were under the influence of the Charlieville Planning Commission.

The purple Volkswagen rolled quietly through the empty streets. It was nearly the only car on the road. Charlieville was a strange place in the middle of the night. Billboards were lit up and neon signs flickered even though no one was awake to look at them. When the purple Volkswagen stopped for a red light, Watson could hear the electricity buzzing and sputtering in the wires overhead. He'd never heard that in the daytime.

The corner of Perry and Magill, one of the biggest intersections in town, was nearly deserted. The traffic lights flashed orange to empty streets in both directions. Once, a police car followed them for a few blocks. Fred Achziger drove carefully and soon the police car turned into the parking lot of an all-night coffee shop.

"Where is this laboratory, anyway?" said Watson. "Unfortunately," said Fred Achziger, "it is on the other side of town."

The other side of town was mostly industrial. There were a lot of factories down there, and nobody around at night but a few artists who lived in warehouses that had been converted into big apartments called lofts.

Without traffic, a trip that might have taken over an hour during the day took them less than half an hour. In this part of town, there were only about three street lights per block. Big black stretches of sidewalk lay between the empty islands of light. Watson's imagination supplied the kind of unsavory characters that might be hanging around in the blots of darkness: murderers and muggers, mostly, he supposed.

This was worse than the forest. Urban blight was something he'd been hearing about all his life. It was one of the things the Charlieville Planning Commission said it was trying to stop. Watson had never before experienced it firsthand.

The purple Volkswagen rounded a corner and parked in a big empty lot that was mostly dirt and rock. Splatters of broken glass shone like diamonds. Watson could see the remains of small islands of asphalt, so the lot must have been paved at one time.

The lot was next to a big brick building that looked even more decrepit than the other buildings that Watson could see. Many of the windows high up in the wall were broken, and the big sign that said FISHBEIN PRODUCTIONS was terribly faded.

When Fred Achziger turned off the car's engine, silence pressed in on them. The silence was more ominous than the sound of the wind and the things that lived in the forest. At least, if a thing made a sound, you could keep track of where it was. The only sound Watson heard was the halfhearted chirping of some crickets. Then, far away, a motor began to chug.

"Well, we're here," Martin Trent said.

"This is it?" asked Watson.

"You should have seen it in its heyday," Fred Achziger said. "Hollywood never had a studio half so glamorous."

"It was swell," Martin Trent said.

They got out of the car and the faraway motor stopped

chugging. Watson felt that except for the crickets, he could have been on the Moon. In fact, he would have preferred being on the Moon. He did not feel safe in this place at this hour.

They walked across the parking lot and around to the front of the building. Watson turned on his Captain Conquer emergency light so they could see what was in the dark patch they had to cross next. There was nothing but a clean stretch of bone-white sidewalk.

"Come along," said Fred Achziger. He led off, keeping his back to the building as he ran sideways across the sidewalk. In the silence of the industrial night, Fred Achziger sounded as if he were tapdancing. So did Watson and Martin Trent as they followed.

They came to a boarded-up door with the words NO TRESPASSING hastily painted on it in black. Martin Trent grabbed the door handle and shook it. The door rattled but seemed solidly locked. "Now what?" Martin Trent said.

"We need a key," Watson said. "That's one thing the Captain Conquer ring doesn't have."

"Perhaps yours doesn't," said Fred Achziger. "But mine...." He held up his genuine styrene metal-tone ring and opened the secret compartment. He shook out something that clanged like a bell when it hit the cement. Martin Trent knelt quickly to pick it up "A key," he said happily, and handed it to Fred Achziger.

Fred Achziger spoke as he brushed away cobwebs and fitted the key into the lock. "I kept it all these years as a memento of the days when Captain Conquer was still in production." The lock gave a decisive click, and while smiling at Watson, Fred Achziger pushed the door open with the palm of one hand. "As a man with forty pounds of brains in his nose, I knew it would be a good thing to do." Watson smiled back at Fred Achziger. Fred Achziger stepped into the darkness beyond the door.

Watson followed him, then stopped just inside. The air was cold and dusty. Watson sneezed twice.

They were in a big room, much like the sound-stage back at Channel 14. In places, the yellowing insulation fell away from the wall in patches, and looked like moss. The catwalks above were as forbidding as the twisted branches of trees back in the forest. Watson wondered if rats lived in this place.

The three made footsteps in the untrodden expanse of the dusty floor and they all sneezed every now and again. The sneezing and the dust and the cold made Watson irritable. He itched in places he could not reach, including inside his body. He began to wonder, as he hadn't wondered for hours, exactly what he was doing with these two crazy old men. He should go to the police. There was nothing wrong with the police. Let the police explore cold dusty warehouses at night. But he kept walking.

He became aware that they were walking toward

big blocky things resting on the floor. At first, they were only like solid places in the darkness, but in a few seconds it became clear that they were really odd-shaped things covered with big tarpaulins.

Fred Achziger strolled over to what appeared to be a high wall. He said, "Please remove the tarp."

Martin Trent grabbed the tarpaulin in both hands. Fred Achziger said, "Gently, Martin. That thing is covered with twenty years of dust." Martin Trent nodded and pulled on the tarpaulin. As careful as Martin Trent was, pulling the tarpaulin off raised a cloud of dust that was nearly atomic in its proportions. All three of them sneezed over and over again. Watson's eyes watered, and for a moment he couldn't see anything, not even dust.

When Watson could see again, he realized what the tarpaulin had been covering. Layers of wood were peeling away from it, and the paint was faded, but the shape was unmistakable. It was a full-size model of Captain Conquer's stratoship, the Great Auk. It didn't have any wings, but Watson could see where they had been attached.

Fred Achziger stood back from the Great Auk, studying it with pleasure. Martin Trent stepped forward and touched the airplane as if it were some kind of religious artifact. He slid his hand along its flaking flank. "I never thought I'd see the Great Auk again," he said.

Watson knocked on the side of the airplane. It sounded hollow. Small things skittered inside.

Rats? Insects? Creepy things in any case. "Well," said Watson as he stepped back from the Great Auk, "here we are. What's supposed to happen now?"

"I don't know," said Fred Achziger. "But we haven't seen everything yet." He walked across a large area that had once been painted white. He walked past walls with windows and electronic gadgets painted on them. The walls did not go all the way to the ceiling. He walked past something else covered with a tarpaulin that might have been a big desk and a high-backed chair. He was walking through Captain Conquer's secret office.

At the other side of the soundstage was what appeared to be the interior of a cave. "Come over here, Watson," said Fred Achziger. "I want you to see this."

Watson crossed through the Captain's office feeling as if not only his surroundings, but he himself, were unreal. He'd been seeing all this stuff on television for years. On television, the Great Auk looked like a real stratoship. The office looked bright and efficient—like a place where great plans might be hatched, great problems might be solved.

But here, standing on a twenty-year-old set, Watson suffered not only from a strange mental double vision, but oddly enough from a certain melancholy disappointment. Captain Conquer's stuff wasn't supposed to look this way.

It was odd. All this time he'd been fighting belief in Captain Conquer, and now, presented with absolute proof of the Captain's falsity, he wanted desperately for the Captain to be real. Watson resented the proof that he was not.

Watson got to where Fred Achziger stood on the cave set. In the bright light, Watson could see where spider webs were spun in the cave's niches, crannies, and cracks. Fred Achziger pulled a tarp off a big square thing to reveal a massive control panel topped by a huge light bulb inside a cross-hatching of thick metal bars.

"Humph," said Fred Achziger.

"What is it?" asked Watson.

"This is the secret underground laboratory of Destructowitz, Master of Time and Space, Captain Conquer's archnemesis." Fred Achziger hit the control panel with the flat of his hand and a small cloud of dust rose. "From this control panel," he said, "Destructowitz, Master of Time and Space, could cause earthquakes, floods, power outages, invasions from space, attacks by dinosaurs. The only thing that stood between him and world domination was Captain Conquer."

"Wow," Watson said, just as if Destructowitz, Master of Time and Space, had been real. Then a question occurred to him. "Did all this stuff come from the Catalog of Raunchypur?"

"Most of it did, yes."

"Then it's all real. It all works."

"If one knows how to make it work."

"Then the guy who played Destructowitz, Master

of Time and Space, could really have dominated the world."

"Don't be silly. That sort of thing takes a man with forty pounds of brains in his nose or a genius like Berkowitz."

"Then you—"

Watson was interrupted by a shout from Martin Trent, who was standing before Captain Conquer's desk. "What is it?" said Fred Achziger as he hurried to join him. Still confused, Watson followed.

Martin Trent said, "I want to see the desk."

"I understand."

"But I wanted you both here when I pulled off the tarp."

"I understand," said Fred Achziger again. "Go ahead."

Barely disturbing the dust, Martin Trent slowly pulled the tarpaulin from Captain Conquer's desk and chair. One side of the desk was covered with toggle switches, and little lights, and a bank of small TV screens. The chair had its back to them.

Martin Trent said, "Do you know how often I stood right about where I'm standing now, ready to take orders, ready to think through a problem, ready—well, ready for anything?"

Watson nodded.

"And the Captain sat right here," Martin Trent said, and put his hand on the chair to turn it around. He slowly swiveled the chair and all three fell back a pace in horror. For in the chair sat a member of the Charlieville Planning Commission. In his hand was a blaster that might have been used by Destructowitz, Master of Time and Space. He was pointing the blaster at them.

"We knew that you would show up sooner or later," said the Commissioner. "Where is Berkowitz?"

"He's not coming," said Fred Achziger.

"No matter. Perhaps Sherlock Congruent can do the job by himself, after all."

"You have my father?" Watson cried.

"We do. And now we have you too. The three of you are awfully nosey. We can't have you running around spoiling our plans."

"You can shoot only one of us before the other two get to you," said Martin Trent.

"I wouldn't say that," said the Commissioner. From the back of Destructowitz's cave came the other four Commissioners, each with his blaster drawn and aimed.

"Oops," said Martin Trent.

"Here we go," the Commissioner said. He held up the hand not holding the blaster to reveal a real metal Captain Conquer ring like Watson's, and pushed a stud on it. Watson could not find a stud like it on his own ring.

For a moment, Watson thought that pushing the stud had started an earthquake. All around them a loud grating noise began, and the floor began to shake. Not so much to shake, actually, as to vibrate.

As he looked from Fred Achziger to Martin Trent, and they looked from each other to him, Watson had the definite impression that the entire building was sinking like a big elevator and taking them with it.

CHAPTER EIGHT
THE PUDDENTAKE FIELD

It was obvious now that the Charlieville Planning Commission was involved in some way with the Puddentakers. Maybe they *were* Puddentakers. Watson had no idea what the aliens looked like, and in any case, a lot of tentacles or claws or whatever could be hidden under the Commissioners' disguise-like clothing.

But if the Charlieville Planning Commission and the Puddentakers had stolen Watson's house and kidnapped his father, why had they left behind the ring and the message? Watson didn't know. When he asked a Planning Commissioner what was going on, the Planning Commissioner said, "Someday, you'll understand."

The studio rumbled and vibrated as it continued to descend. Watson, Fred Achziger, and Martin Trent sat vibrating together on the couch in the Captain's office. The Planning Commissioners watched them and did not seem to get tired of aiming their blasters at them.

"What's that?" Martin Trent said.

Fred Achziger held his nose in the air as he had in the forest and said, "Hmm."

Now Watson could hear it too, a low rhythmic thrumming sound, as if powerful machines were working below. "It's getting louder," he said. A moment later, he said, "Morlocks."

"What's that?" said Martin Trent.

Fred Achziger nodded. "Creatures in H. G. Wells' novel *The Time Machine*. They lived underground and cared for great machines that sounded just like that."

"Not so terrible," said Martin Trent.

"And," Fred Achziger went on, "they captured and ate the people who lived on the surface."

Martin Trent looked at Watson in horror. Watson shrugged.

"Not Morlocks," said one of the Commissioners. "Motivators."

"Why motivators?" said Fred Achziger.

"Someday, you will understand."

With a jolt, the studio stopped descending and suddenly the big overhead lights came on. Watson switched off his ring. The motivators sounded as if they were all around the studio, right outside its walls. Watson could not stop thinking about Morlocks.

The Commissioners backed toward the door brandishing their blasters at Watson, Fred Achziger, and Martin Trent. One of the Commissioners said, "Wait here. Someone will come for you soon."

"For what?" said Watson. "And where's my father?"

"Someday, you will understand."

When they were gone, Martin Trent ran across the floor and tried the door. It was locked. He looked back at Fred Achziger and said, "You didn't tell them you have forty pounds of brains in your nose."

"They did not seem the type to be impressed."

"Probably not," said Martin Trent as he walked dejectedly back to Captain Conquer's office and threw himself into the Captain's chair. He said, "What do we do now?"

From his ring, Fred Achziger pulled the minuscule deck of cards and slapped them down on Captain Conquer's desk. Martin Trent waved away the dust that rose. Fred Achziger said, "Anybody for a hot game of cards?"

"Go Fish?" said Martin Trent.

"Perfect," said Fred Achziger.

"I don't believe you two," said Watson. "We should be looking for a way out of here, making plans to rescue my father. Something!"

"How do you know that I am not?" said Fred Achziger.

"Because you're playing cards," Watson said with exasperation.

Fred Achziger tapped the side of his nose.

"All right," said Watson. "You guys play cards. I'll look around."

Fred Achziger began to deal the cards.

Watson walked across the dusty floor, now marked with the footprints and scuffings of many people, to the door through which they'd come, and began to feel his way around the walls. He banged and he thumped and he pressed and he shook panels that seemed to be loose. Nothing became a doorway.

He heard a noise inside the wall. He stopped banging, and put his ear up against the wire mesh. Something inside or beyond the wall was moving. Seconds later, a scratching sound began almost at his feet. Watson ran to get Fred Achziger and Martin Trent.

"Do you have any fives?" Fred Achziger said.

"Nary a one," said Martin Trent. "Go fish."

"Something's coming through the wall!" cried Watson.

"What?" Fred Achziger and Martin Trent followed him back to the wall and listened attentively.

"Rats?" said Martin Trent.

"Gophers," said Fred Achziger.

"How do you know?" Watson asked. As he spoke, a nose bristling with whiskers pushed aside a piece of soundproofing. It was not long before a gopher stared up at the three, looked around the big room, and backed out again.

"Berkowitz's gophers," said Fred Achziger. "He uses them for reconnaissance."

"We must be miles from his ticket booth," said Watson.

"This is not one of the gophers we saw there," said Fred Achziger. "But Berkowitz has his ways of communicating with them, no matter how far away they are."

Watson thought of the headdress made of aluminum foil and hangers that Berkowitz had been wearing. "If the gophers can get out, maybe we can too." Watson got down on his knees and lifted the soundproofing to see where the gopher had gone. The hole was small and dark and not much bigger than a rain gutter. Watson shone his Captain Conquer light into the opening. Light glinted off eyes that blinked once and were gone.

An unfamiliar voice said, "You clowns will never escape that way."

The three of them looked around and saw a man standing by the door with his hand on the knob. He wore a tattered green jumpsuit with food stains on the front. On his face was at least three days' growth of gray grizzled beard. "Who are you?" Fred Achziger said.

The stranger said, "How soon they forget," and walked casually, as if he owned the place, across the floor toward Captain Conquer's office. Watson thought he recognized the voice, but could not place it. It was as if he had heard the voice in a dream, or a long time before.

The man plopped himself into Captain Conquer's

chair and leaned back in it with his big heavy army boots up on the desk.

"Get your feet off that desk," said Martin Trent threateningly.

Fred Achziger had not yet moved. He said, "If I didn't have forty pounds of brains in my nose, I wouldn't believe it."

"Hey," said the object of Fred Achziger's disbelief, as Martin Trent lifted the man's feet and threw them to the floor. "Nobody has more right to put his feet on that desk than I do," the stranger cried, and stood up. "Isn't that right, Martin?"

Martin Trent peered at him, then pulled back as if the man had suddenly turned green. "Webb," said Martin, "is that you?"

"It ain't Destructowitz, Master of Time and Space."

Watson did not quite know what to think of this grubby old man, and Martin Trent seemed to be in shock. Fred Achziger crossed the room with his hand extended, took the fellow's hand in his and shook it with enthusiasm. "I'd know you anywhere, Webb. How are you? Long time no see." Then he suddenly let go of the hand, hit his own chest with one fist, and opened it as he brought it around in front of him.

The man had a quirky self-satisfied smile on his face as he made the same salute at Fred Achziger.

"This is Captain Conquer?" Watson said with some amazement.

"Have a little respect for your elders, kid," he said,

but he was still smiling.

"Webb," said Fred Achziger, "this is Sherlock Congruent's boy, Watson."

"Sherlock? Isn't that the guy the Puddentakers have building motivators for them?" Webb Washington took Martin Trent by the arm and guided him to the big chair. "You better sit down before you fall down, Chuckles," Webb Washington said. Martin Trent sat down, but he never took his eyes off Webb Washington.

"Can you get us out of here?" said Watson.

Webb Washington strolled slowly around the room. He said, "I could. But I won't."

"Why not?" said Watson.

"That's a long story." Webb Washington turned to Fred Achziger. "Still have thirty-five pounds of brains in your nose?" he said.

"Forty now," said Fred Achziger. "Where have you been all these years?"

"Right here." Webb Washington flicked some flaking paint off the Great Auk. "A couple of weeks after we stopped production, the Puddentakers contacted me."

"The same aliens who run the Raunchypur Catalog?" said Watson.

"Smart kid," said Webb Washington. He continued his stroll around the studio. "Anyway, the Puddentakers are big fans of the show. They know I'm just an actor, but they don't mind. They like to have me around anyway." As if he were some kind of building inspector, he picked up one edge of some old soundproofing and looked at the wall beneath. He winked at Watson. "It's a living," he said.

Watson said, "But what has the Charlieville Planning Commission to do with all this? And what do they want with motivators, anyway? And why won't you help us?"

Webb Washington strolled slowly back toward them. He said, "Because the members of the Charlieville Planning Commission are Puddentakers too."

"Well, that explains—" Watson suddenly stopped talking. He shook his head. "It doesn't explain anything." He shook his head again. He was really disappointed that this old guy was Captain Conquer. Now that Watson knew who he was, Webb Washington did look like a stooped, wrinkled, white-haired version of the straight and strong hero he saw on television. Could he be of any more help than Fred Achziger or Martin Trent or Berkowitz?

Watson said, "I have a message for you from Alvin Algae."

"Oh?" said Webb Washington. He sat on the corner of the desk, with one foot on the floor and the other foot swinging. "How is old moneybags?"

"He's fine. But he and a lot of other people are looking for you. They want to make a Captain Conquer movie."

"They do, huh?" Webb Washington laughed once, bitterly. "Well, I'm not going anywhere. Alvin Algae can go whistle for me."

"What about my father?"

"What about him?"

Fred Achziger said, "Watson has come a long way to see you. You are a great hero to him. Surely—"

"Surely, nothing." Webb Washington poked Fred Achziger in the chest with one finger. "Listen: I always wanted to be a super-hero when I was a kid. When I grew up, I discovered there were no such things as super-heroes so I settled for *pretending* to be a super-hero. It was fun, but I got tired of it. When I was kidnapped some years ago by the aliens of Puddentake, they made me their mascot. They treat me well. Better than Alvin Algae ever treated me. I'm happy here."

"But—" said Watson.

Webb Washington glared at Watson. "I ain't finished yet, kid." He went on: "In exchange for their taking care of me, all I have to do is make an occasional personal appearance, or introduce the cartoons they sometimes show. I like it here. I don't want to upset the applecart. I learned there ain't no such thing as a super-hero. It's time for you to grow up too, kid."

"*Me* grow up!" Watson shouted. He looked accusingly at Fred Achziger and Martin Trent. Martin Trent was still in shock, but Fred Achziger looked away. Watson tried to calm himself. He took a deep breath and said, "Even if you're not a super-hero, you could still help."

"Yeah, I could, but I won't. If I won't upset the applecart to save the entire planet Earth, why should I do it to save your father?"

Martin Trent snapped out of his trance. He said, "But why should the entire planet Earth need saving?"

"How you doing, Martin?" Webb Washington said.

"I'd feel better if you'd help us."

"Yeah, well, the entire planet needs saving because the Puddentakers plan to use the Puddentake Field on it."

"What's—?" began Martin Trent, but Webb Washington held up his hand to silence him.

"The Puddentake Field," said Webb Washington, "will make the Earth just like the aliens' planet, Puddentake, so their own people can live here. The Puddentake Field will turn the atmosphere of the Earth into stuff almost exactly like something that is not quite the same as cold cherry Jell-O. The inspection committee from Puddentake will arrive soon. If the Puddenforming isn't done by that time, the Planning Commission will be in big trouble. But there shouldn't be a problem—" Webb Washington smiled slyly—"with your father helping them."

"Dad would never do a thing like that," said Watson.

"Maybe not. But he's building their motivators."

"Excuse me," said Fred Achziger. "But what

will they do with the motivators?"

Webb Washington took a deep breath. He said, "All right, listen up 'cause I'm only gonna say this once: The Puddentakers have hollowed out all the area under Charlieville. That's why it's so easy to lower buildings into the ground. Anyway, they've set the entire town on an undercarriage supported by enormous wheels. You'll probably see them after a while. The motivators your father is building are much bigger than the ones that power the Great Auk—taller even than Fred Achziger."

"I'm not surprised," Fred Achziger said. "The square/cube law, you know."

"Uh-huh," said Watson. "Go on."

"Like I say, your father's motivators are really big, and more powerful than anything the Puddentakers have been able to come up with themselves. But they have to be to carry the entire city of Charlieville across the desert to Hampton, the town at the other end of the valley."

"But—?" said Martin Trent. Webb Washington stopped him again by raising his hand.

"You see, each city is designed as half a circuit board, using city streets, phone and power lines as energy ducts, diodes, capacitors, transistors, and other electronic garbage."

Watson said, "So that's why the Planning Commission was always tearing up the streets and doing strange things like putting a telephone pole in Mrs. Ferguson's back yard."

"Exactly."

"But?" said Martin Trent again. He did not go on.

"Good question, Martin. When the two halves of the circuit board come together, the aliens will be able to generate the Puddentake Field."

"Why two halves?" said Watson.

"It was a matter of national security, I'm sure," said Fred Achziger.

"Right."

Watson folded his arms and said, "This all sounds as flaky as the paint on the Great Auk."

"You'll see," said Webb Washington.

"You don't seem very disturbed by all this," said Martin Trent.

"I'm not. The Puddentakers are going to give me a planet all to myself. Someplace where they never heard of Captain Conquer."

"You've changed," said Fred Achziger. "You used to embody the Captain's high ideals, even off the set and out of uniform."

"Yeah, well, that's a long time ago. I've learned a lot about life since then."

"Aw, Captain," Martin Trent said.

Fred Achziger said, "Rather, I think you have forgotten a lot."

"And he's lying about my father," said Watson.

Webb Washington shook his head. "Sorry, kid," he said.

There was a commotion at the other side of the room. It sounded as if someone had just spilled a truckload of tin cans. Suddenly the door swung open, and a line of robots entered. Each one looked as if it were actually made of tin cans—a big one for the body, a smaller one for the head, and even smaller ones connected to make up arms and legs. Each foot looked like an old electric iron. On top of each robot's head was a red vacuum tube protected by a wire cage. The robots had no noses.

The lead robot looked at them through round eye sensors that glowed a dull orange. Through jagged teeth, the lead robot spoke in a nasal whine, like someone who had a cold. It said, "Come with us." It pointed its finger at Watson and Fred Achziger and Martin Trent. Its finger seemed to be the barrel of a blaster.

"Better go," said Webb Washington. "These guys aren't programmed for patience."

CHAPTER NINE
THROW OUT THE INTERLOCKS!

The robots ignored Webb Washington. He sauntered along behind as Watson, Fred Achziger, and Martin Trent were herded out of the Fishbein Studios and into a hallway whose boundaries were defined by light that fell from fluorescent tubes overhead. The only wall that Watson could see was the side of the Fishbein Studios building, and that, of course, ended less than a block away.

In the distance, Watson saw other hallways of light. And still farther away, even more hallways of light. They ran side by side and crossed each other, seemingly into infinity. It was easy to believe that all the space under Charlieville had been hollowed out.

The sound of a hardware store in motion that the robots made when they moved could not drown out the rumble of the motivators. It sounded like a bowling ball rolling along forever, becoming louder and softer again each time it encountered a seam in the floor.

In the enormous darkness between the hallways, in the enormous audible range above the thrumming of the motivators, between the clinking and clanking of the robots, Watson heard the skittering sounds of small, quick animals moving around. Perhaps they were gophers sent by Berkowitz. Watson hoped so.

As the group walked along the uneven rock floor, Watson noticed that the fluorescent tubes were attached to wide, thick metal I-beams—the kind used to build bridges. They were full of rivets. Watson nudged Fred Achziger and pointed to them. Fred Achziger nodded and said, "Yes. No doubt part of the undercarriage that Webb spoke of."

"There must be wheels the size of houses around here someplace."

"I would guess that they are out there in the darkness. It doesn't take a man who has forty pounds of brains in his nose to see that if the wheels were in the hallways they would just be in the way."

Watson agreed. He tried not to think about the weight of an entire town being above his head.

They came to a cross hallway. "I'll look in on you once you're settled," Webb Washington called after them as the robots steered Watson, Fred Achziger, and Martin Trent to the left.

"Don't bother," said Martin Trent. He was no longer in shock. But he looked so despondent that it seemed every muscle in his face drooped.

"Chuckles, I...," said Webb Washington. Watson looked back at him. He seemed lonely standing there at the intersection, and he didn't know what to do with his hands.

"He's a great disappointment to you, isn't he?"

said Fred Achziger.

Martin Trent tried to smile, but the expression was not very convincing. He shrugged. "Naw. Just a TV show. The guy's only human."

Watson and Fred Achziger looked at each other and shook their heads.

It wasn't long before Watson saw an enormous cube that, at one edge, touched the hallway they were walking along. It rose between the girders until it was lost in the darkness above them. As they approached, Watson concluded that the cube was really the bottom floor of a building. He wondered if any of the building still showed on the surface.

The wall of the building looked very old. It was made of brick that had cracks and stains all over it. Pipes and electrical conduits clung to the wall like some kind of industrial ivy.

The robots stopped Watson and Fred Achziger and Martin Trent before a gray metal door in the wall. Three people could have walked through it easily had it been open. The sound of the motivators had never been so loud. It almost seemed as if the sound were inside Watson's head, trying to get out. The motivators were probably right behind that door.

One of the robots stepped forward and swung a metal bar away from where it had been lodged. With both hands—its fingers seemed to be made of thimbles—the robot grabbed the thick horizontal handle and pulled open the door. The hinges made a long teeth-jarring squeal.

They went into the big dark bottom floor of the building and Watson was hit by the humming of the motivators. The sound was almost strong enough to lean against. Like the dramatic music in movies or TV shows, the insistence of the rhythm made Watson feel that something awful was coming, or that a terrible event was about to happen. Work lights with shades like coolie hats swung from the ceiling, making the shadows of the big shapes move as if they were dancing bears. Watson knew that the shapes were motivators, because they looked like electric fans with the fan part encased in metal, just like the one on his father's workbench back home. There were hundreds of them in the big room, lined up in rows.

The robots escorted Watson, Fred Achziger, and Martin Trent back among the motivators. The temperature rose as they walked, and soon Watson was sweating. Also, there was a strange smell in the air. It wasn't unpleasant, but Watson couldn't identify it. It got stronger as they walked.

When they reached the other end of the building, Watson saw why the air had been getting warmer. Built into the brick wall was a big metal door open to reveal a furnace in full roar. The furnace looked like a whole city of fire. Flames sometimes licked out the big metal door as if the fire were a hungry animal trying to escape. The heat was intense. Watson still didn't know what the unusual odor was, but now it smelled like burning candy bars.

In front of the metal door were three robots who took turns scooping shovelfuls of brown granules from a big mound and chucking them into the furnace. When they did this, the fire roared louder for a few seconds and more flame licked out the open metal doors. The candy-bar smell was suddenly stronger.

One of the robot escorts flashed its red light at the three robot shovelers. Each shoveler flashed back, then handed one of the captives a shovel and joined the escort group. While Fred Achziger, Watson, and Martin Trent stood there with shovels in their hands, another robot said in its whiny voice, "Now you shovel." No one moved. The robot shouted, "Now!" and raised its blaster finger.

As slowly as they dared, Fred Achziger, Martin Trent, and Watson each lifted a shovelful of the brown stuff and chucked it into the furnace. They were all sweating now, and the firelight shone on their wet skins. Big wet splotches grew under their arms, across their chests and down their backs.

One of the robots stood motionless, watching them, while the rest of the robots marched off. As they slowly shoveled the brown granules, Watson, Fred Achziger, and Martin Trent listened to the robots cross the room and slam the door on the far side of the motivators.

Fred Achziger and Martin Trent were starting to breathe hard. Neither one was as young as he used to be. Watson's muscles hurt. He was not really in very good physical shape. They were all a little sloppy with the brown stuff, but the robot didn't seem to mind as long as they kept moving. Watson said, "We'll be shoveling this stuff for the rest of our lives."

"You forget Berkowitz," Fred Achziger said. He wiped his forehead with his arm. His purple suit, so grand at his retirement party, now looked as if he'd stolen it from some street person.

"Yeah, Berkowitz," Martin Trent said. "The Captain won't help us. But we've still got Berkowitz. Ol' Berkowitz'll come through for us." Martin Trent sounded a little crazy. It was obvious that the shock of finding out the truth about Webb Washington had been very hard on him.

Watson picked up a shovelful of brown granules, brought it close to his eyes and looked at it by the uneven firelight. He sniffed it. It smelled like chocolate. "What is this stuff anyway?" he asked.

Fred Achziger said, "It's Chocolatron."

"Chocolatron!" cried Watson.

"Of course. We are shoveling it into the atomic furnace that makes the motivators go."

"Go? But the city isn't moving."

"No." Fred Achziger slowly shoveled Chocolatron for a while. Then he said, "As a man with forty pounds of brains in his nose, I guess that the Puddentakers must have Charlieville running in neutral until they're ready to make the run across the desert to Hampton."

Martin Trent said, "I hope Berkowitz finds us before that happens. Wherever we are." He looked around warily as he shoveled Chocolatron.

"I know exactly where we are," Fred Achziger said. Watson and Martin Trent stopped to look at him. The robot shifted its weight and lifted its blaster finger. "Keep shoveling," it said in its funny nasal voice.

The three looked at the robot angrily, but there was no arguing with it. "Where?" asked Martin Trent as he lifted another load of Chocolatron.

"We are," said Fred Achziger, "in the sub-basement of the Warehouse of Raunchypur."

"How do you know?" said Watson.

"Forty pounds of brains, I expect," said Martin Trent.

"Not at all," said Fred Achziger. "I used to work in this warehouse part-time when I was in high school. We didn't come down to the sub-basement very often, but I remember it well."

Watson knitted his eyebrows. "You mean," he said with growing excitement, "that all those time machines and blasters and warp engines are available just over our heads?"

"Yes," said Fred Achziger calmly. "As a matter of fact, I recognize these robots themselves as a Raunchypur product."

"Let's get up there and use that equipment to stop the Puddentakers," Watson said eagerly.

"Yes, yes," said Fred Achziger. "If we can get away from our guard, and if we can get upstairs, and if the equipment is charged and ready. Which for safety reasons it most assuredly will not be."

"But—" Watson began. He was interrupted by the sound of the metal door at the other side of the room being unbarred. It squeaked open. Metal feet marched in and came closer.

"We'll be shoveling Chocolatron forever if we don't do something," Watson whispered.

"I don't think so," said Fred Achziger. "Depend on Berkowitz and my forty pounds of brains."

Watson looked heavenward for strength and imagined he could see the Raunchypur super-science weapons through the dirty ceiling. "Shovel!" whined the robot.

Soon the other robots arrived and flashed the red lights on the tops of their heads at the guard. The guard flashed back and went to join the others. Watson, Fred Achziger, and Martin Trent took this opportunity to rest on their shovels.

One of the robots pointed its blaster finger at Watson and said, "Come with us." All three put down their shovels. "Not you two," said the robot, pointing at Fred Achziger and Martin Trent. "You," it said, pointing at Watson again. Watson looked pleadingly at Fred Achziger.

"Where are you taking him?" Fred Achziger asked.

"You two shovel," said a robot. It remained

to guard Fred Achziger and Martin Trent while another robot grabbed Watson in an iron grip—which is what he would have expected from a robot—and pulled him away. Watson cried, "Help me, Fred!"

"Shovel," said the robot guard.

"I'm working on it," Fred Achziger called to Watson as his shovel crunched into the mound of Chocolatron.

The robot guided Watson through the sub-basement of the Warehouse of Raunchypur and out the door into the hallway of light. All the while, Watson thought nasty thoughts about Berkowitz and forty pounds of brains.

* * * * * * *

The robots herded him through the maze of hallways. They seemed to walk for a long time. The Puddentakers had not lowered many buildings into the ground, so Watson had few reference points to tell him where he was. They could have been on the other side of Charlieville by now.

Everywhere they went, Watson heard the movements of small animals. A couple of times he thought he saw gophers. Watson couldn't tell if they belonged to Berkowitz or not.

Then, in the distance, he saw a familiar building. As they walked closer, the robots banging around like silverware in a cement mixer, Watson became more certain of what it was. He whooped with joy and struggled to get away from the robots, but he needn't have bothered. They stopped right in front of the building. It was the house with two front doors, his own home.

He just stood there, drawing pleasure and strength from looking at it. One of the robots said, "Go in." From inside, Watson heard what sounded like a dinosaur shrieking. "Dad!" Watson cried. The robot didn't have to tell him twice.

Watson ran through the Captain Conquer PX and into the back room. His father was just turning away from his workbench. He smiled broadly when he saw Watson. They jumped at each other and hugged. "I never thought I'd see you again," Watson said. He felt all soft and warm inside.

"Why?" said Mr. Congruent. "Didn't you get my message?"

Watson stepped back from him and said, "What message?"

"In the ring. In the metal Captain Conquer ring I left for you where our house used to be."

"*You* left that ring?" Watson was astonished. He sat back on a stool. He noticed that a gopher was sleeping on the workbench next to the oscilloscope.

"Why sure. Who did you think would leave it?"

"The Charlieville Planning Commission."

Now Mr. Congruent sat down. He said, "What made you think they left it?"

"They were waiting for us at the Fishbein Studios," Watson said.

"Huh," Mr. Congruent said. "I didn't know they could read the Captain's code." He shook his head.

"But if the members of the Planning Commission are Puddentakers, you should have guessed."

"You know, come to think of it, I did guess that. But it didn't seem important. It never occurred to me that they would *want* to read my coded message."

Now that Watson knew his father was safe, he felt a little angry at him. "Why did you have to be so secretive?"

"Well, mainly because I didn't want the Puddentakers to take Berkowitz instead of me. You see, we both know almost the same amount about the Captain and his devices. But I thought it would be nice to work *with* Berkowitz."

"You could have told me that."

"There wasn't time."

Watson thought about that for a moment. He was still angry, but the anger was fading. He knew that his father always meant well. Staying angry would only make them both feel bad. He noticed that another gopher was watching them from the floor beneath the workbench. Watson said, "But why in code?"

"Oh, it seemed like the right thing to do. Captain Conquer himself used to leave a message like that at the end of every show. Besides, I thought it might pique your curiosity."

"Unlike the fact that both my father and our house were missing."

Mr. Congruent shrugged and smiled shyly. "I thought a little mystery might be fun," he said.

To tell the truth, Watson was confused. He had just been through the strangest experiences of his life because his father thought a little mystery might be fun. He felt that he'd been put to a lot of trouble for nothing. With the right message, he could have just found Berkowitz and taken him to the Fishbein Studios, or anywhere else. (How they would have gotten down into the space under Charlieville was another matter. Watson was confident they would have found a way.)

Trouble or fun? Hadn't Watson been complaining just the other day that he was bored because nothing exciting ever happened to him? Hadn't his father given him almost more excitement than he could handle? Maybe, even without knowing it, Mr. Congruent had done the right thing. Everything was all right now. Except for a few small matters.

Watson said, "Yeah, well, I guess you're right. You remember the genuine metal-tone styrene plastic Captain Conquer ring you gave me for my birthday?"

"Of course. I hope you're enjoying it."

"Well, actually, I don't have it on me. It's in my locker at school. It kinda fell on the floor and broke."

"Oh." Mr. Congruent looked at the floor.

"I didn't do it on purpose," Watson said.

"I'm sure you didn't." Mr. Congruent shook himself as if shaking off a bad dream and said, "Well, it doesn't matter. That metal ring you have now is much sturdier." He put his hand on Watson's shoulder and said, "I'm just glad you're here and safe. Why don't you go take a nap or something? I have to get back to work."

"That's the other thing," Watson said gravely. "Webb Washington told us what you're doing for the Puddentakers."

"Us? You and who else?"

"Fred Achziger and Martin Trent helped me find you."

"Well, well, good old Fred and Martin. I hope I'll be seeing them soon."

"Right now they're shoveling Chocolatron into the atomic furnace that runs the motivators."

"What? I know that the atomic furnace needs constant attention or it would go out in less than an hour, but usually a few of the robots handle the shoveling."

"If you're surprised at what Fred Achziger and Martin Trent are doing, just think how surprised I was to find out that you are building motivators for the Puddentakers."

"Surprised? Why?"

Watson told Mr. Congruent what he had heard from Webb Washington about the Puddentakers using the Puddentake Field to turn the atmosphere of the Earth into stuff almost exactly like something that is not quite the same as cold cherry Jell-O.

"I don't believe it," Mr. Congruent said.

"You know how sinister the Planning Commission

looks. And all the strange things they've done over the years. It's possible that Webb Washington is lying, but I don't think so."

Mr. Congruent shook his head. "And all the time I thought the Puddentakers were just big fans of Captain Conquer."

"According to Webb Washington, they're that too. But that doesn't keep them from wanting to take over the Earth."

"I guess not. Well, I've stopped working on the project as of now." He leaned over and switched off the oscilloscope. "There's only one thing I don't understand. If Webb Washington—also known as Captain Conquer—knows about the Puddentakers' plot, why doesn't he do something about it?"

Watson looked at the gopher under the workbench. It winked at him. Or did it just have a tic? Watson didn't know. He also didn't know how to tell his father that Webb Washington was not quite the stalwart human being Mr. Congruent thought he was. Still, Mr. Congruent had asked the question and it had to be answered.

Watson said slowly, "I think there are some things about Webb Washington that you ought to know." He told his father about how Webb Washington's goal in life was not to upset the applecart.

"He's just pretending. Why, I remember how in one episode—'The Jackalope Rebellion,' I think it was— when he pretended to be a bad guy. He even went so far as to—"

"He wasn't pretending this time, Dad. I was there. I heard him talking. Webb Washington is just a broken-down old actor with no concern for anybody but himself. He isn't Captain Conquer anymore. If he ever was."

"He's smarter than you think."

"Maybe. He told me to grow up and not believe in super-heroes anymore. Maybe we both should take his advice."

Quietly, Mr. Congruent said, "You have to believe in something, Watson."

Watson didn't know what to say to that. He and his father sat for a long time without saying anything. The gopher who had been sleeping on the workbench yawned mightily and scratched behind his ear with a back foot, thumping the workbench as he did so.

The bell over the outside door tinkled and both of them looked up. Somebody was walking through the Captain Conquer PX. There were no clinking-clanking sounds, so Watson didn't think it was a robot. A hand pushed aside the green curtain, and standing there in the doorway was Webb Washington himself. He looked kind of sick and sad.

Webb Washington said, "Just a broken-down old actor, huh, kid?"

Watson and Mr. Congruent were both astonished. "How did you know I said that?" said Watson.

"Captain Conquer has his ways," said Webb

Washington.

Mr. Congruent suddenly brightened. "You picked up our conversation on Destructowitz's machine," he said.

"How else?" said Webb Washington. "If I tuned it right, I could pick up a conversation on the other side of the world. You're quite a guy, Mr. Congruent. Too bad you got such a creep for a son."

Watson shook his head and said, "Think about it, Dad. Would Captain Conquer say a thing like that?"

"He must have his reasons." Mr. Congruent looked pleadingly at Webb Washington.

"You're a hard case, Mr. Congruent. You really believe in me. Maybe I make a better super-hero than I thought."

"There's still time to help us stop the Puddentakers," said Watson.

Webb Washington squinted and rubbed his chin. "Maybe."

"You see," said Mr. Congruent triumphantly.

The doorbell tinkled as a commotion in the other room began. It sounded as if hundreds of people had all entered at once and were shouting excitedly at the tops of their voices.

Webb Washington looked over his shoulder. Watson and Mr. Congruent looked past him into the PX. Hundreds, maybe thousands of gophers were milling all over the floor and counter tops. They weren't hurting anything, but they seemed awfully excited. They were making clicking noises at each other.

Berkowitz stood in the center of the room with a baseball bat in his upraised hand. On one side of him stood Fred Achziger. On the other side stood Martin Trent. Behind them was a crowd of old people. Some of them carried baseball bats, others had hockey sticks, or tennis rackets, or golf clubs. They all looked ready for anything. When Berkowitz saw Webb Washington, he cried, "Reinforcements!" He smiled broadly.

Watson and Mr. Congruent pushed Webb Washington into the PX. "What's going on here?" Mr. Congruent asked.

Fred Achziger said, "Berkowitz has come at last with the reinforcements. They've just arrived from the Modern Methuselah Rest Home. They effected the daring rescue of Martin and myself, and now we are all here to save the Earth."

"How did he know where to come?" asked Watson.

"Obvious," said Fred Achziger. "He followed the gophers."

Berkowitz flicked the wire-hanger antennas on his headdress and made them vibrate. He said, "Children of the Earth! What music *they* make!"

The old people from the Modern Methuselah Rest Home cheered.

"What do we do now?" said Mr. Congruent.

"Captain Conquer will know," said Berkowitz.

Everybody looked at Webb Washington expectantly. Fred Achziger crossed his arms. Martin Trent turned away and sniffed. Webb Washington looked nervous.

"Well," said Watson. "Does Captain Conquer know or not?"

Webb Washington turned his head from one eager face to the next, looking everyone in the eye. He looked at Martin Trent for a long time. Then he said, "I guess I do."

Everybody cheered again. This time, Fred Achziger and Watson and Mr. Congruent joined in. Martin Trent looked at Webb Washington. He had not cheered along with the others. Seriously, he said, "Captain, do you have a plan?"

Webb Washington laughed and said, "Not unless you brought one of our writers with you." Martin Trent shook his head.

Webb Washington saw this and said, "But I think that my assistant, Chuckles, will agree. The time has come to throw out the interlocks!"

Everybody cheered again. This time they kept it up while Martin Trent walked forward and warmly shook Webb Washington's hand. Watson walked across to shake hands with Fred Achziger. He whispered in Fred Achziger's ear, "I've heard Captain Conquer say 'throw out the interlocks' on his show, but what does it mean?"

Fred Achziger whispered back, "Nobody knows. But whenever Captain Conquer had a problem that the writers couldn't solve, that's what they told him to say."

"Then we're still in big trouble."

Fred Achziger was about to answer when suddenly, the rumble of the motivators rose into a shriek. The room gave a terrific shake, and everyone was thrown to the floor. The room did not shake again, but it continued to vibrate. It made the gophers crazy. They ran around looking for places to hide, but there weren't any.

"What's going on?" cried Martin Trent.

Fred Achziger said, "If there was ever a time to throw out the interlocks, I'm sure this is it. I believe that the Puddentakers have shifted the town out of neutral. Charlieville is now rolling toward its date with destiny."

CHAPTER TEN
CAPTAIN CONQUER RETURNS

The gophers were squealing, and everyone was still on the floor, afraid that if they stood up they'd be knocked over again. A few of the old people from the Modern Methuselah Rest Home were on their hands and knees, shaking their heads as if to clear them.

Stiffly, Webb Washington got to his feet and said, "It's too late. I wouldn't know an interlock if it bit me."

Fred Achziger was still on the floor. He was leaning on one elbow as if he were at a picnic. He looked around and spoke calmly, as if nothing had happened. "Not at all. As a man who has forty pounds of brains in his nose, I know that there is still time to stop the Puddentakers from turning on the Puddentake Field."

"How?" asked Martin Trent. He was clutching the rack of fan magazines to keep his balance.

"I'm working on it," said Fred Achziger. He tapped the side of his nose.

Watson had heard that before. He helped his

father to his feet, and the two of them made sure that no one was badly hurt.

"Aha!" Fred Achziger said as he lifted his finger into the air. "There must be a control room from which the Charlieville Planning Commission steers the town and controls the Puddentake Field. We'll get in there, and make sure the Puddentake Field is never activated."

"I know where that room is," said Webb Washington.

"Very good," said Fred Achziger. "I suggest that you and Watson come with me. Perhaps Martin and his friends from the Modern Methuselah Rest Home would like to see if they can't do something about those pesky robots."

"Like what?" said Berkowitz.

"Like, well, hmm." Fred Achziger began to tap the side of his nose again.

"Feed them liver," Webb Washington said. Everybody laughed. Even Fred Achziger chuckled. Nobody would tell Watson why.

An old woman dressed in a purple flower-print dress had been looking out the door. She raised her hockey stick and cried, "Here come the robots!"

The robots swarmed into the room, swinging their blaster fingers around to cover the crowd. "Back to the atomic furnace," one of the robots whined.

"I—" said Webb Washington, and stopped.

No one in the room moved. Watson watched the

robots as they continued to menace everyone with their blaster fingers. Suddenly, the red lights on the robots' heads gave Watson an idea. "Quick, everybody," he cried. "Blow the whistle feature of your Captain Conquer rings as loud as you can."

"Of course," said Fred Achziger. He blew on his ring and made a loud shrill noise. The robots looked around in confusion. Everybody else put their rings to their lips and blew. The noise was deafening. The PX sounded full of lunatic birds.

But it was worth standing the skull-shattering din because as the terrible noises went on, first singly, then in bunches, the red lights in the little cages on the robot's heads shattered. The humans had to hold their hands and arms before their faces to protect their eyes from flying glass. Soon, there wasn't an unbroken red light in the place.

The robots wandered around aimlessly now, just kind of strolling. Sometimes one of them would run into a counter or a wall, or even another robot. When a robot ran into anything, it bowed slightly, said "Excuse me," and wandered off in another direction.

"Very well," said Fred Achziger. "We have found a way to defeat the robots, but there is much work left to do. Martin, you and Berkowitz take the reinforcements from the Modern Methuselah Rest Home and look for other robots. Webb, Watson, and I will nab the Commissioners in their den, as it were."

"And it were," Webb Washington said.

"What about me?" said Mr. Congruent.

"You stay here and pretend to be working on motivators. Perhaps the Puddentakers will not notice they've been invaded till it's too late for them."

"But won't they notice when we nab them in their den?" said Watson. "Won't they notice when their robots don't check in?"

"Our enemy is wily and powerful. But they have no brains in their noses."

Martin Trent nodded.

"While we're gone," Fred Achziger continued, "perhaps Berkowitz would be good enough to attempt communicating with the inspectors from Puddentake."

"Is that a good idea?" asked Martin Trent.

"Certainly. I want them plenty angry at their own people by the time they arrive. If Berkowitz were not here, I would call them myself on Destructowitz's machine."

"Before you go," said Martin Trent, "I have something I want to give to Webb." He handed Webb Washington a Captain Conquer ring. "I got it from the Catalog of Raunchypur back when we were doing the show. Maybe you can use it against the Puddentakers. It's not just plastic. It's metal, just like Watson's."

Webb Washington put on the ring and nodded to Martin Trent. They shook hands again.

Fred Achziger looked around hurriedly and raised one finger in the air. "And now we must be off," he said. "We must hurry if we are to stop the Puddentakers from using their field to destroy the Earth."

* * * * * * *

Watson and Fred Achziger followed Webb Washington down tunnels of light. Their path turned and twisted, and Watson was glad to have a native guide. While they walked, they discussed what they would do when they confronted the Charlieville Planning Commission. The whine of the motivators became even more shrill. "They've increased their speed," said Fred Achziger. "We must be close to Hampton."

Once they ran into a contingent of robots, but one long piercing whistle from their rings had the robots wandering off into the darkness.

At last they came to a huge cube, which, like the Warehouse of Raunchypur, rose into the darkness between the iron I-beams of the superstructure. Unlike the warehouse, this cube had a smooth metal skin that gleamed in the light of the hallway. One robot stood guard before a pair of red doors. One of the robot's toes flapped against the floor as the city continued to vibrate. Webb Washington said, "Hi, Curly."

"Ha, ha," said the robot. Like the other robots, he had a red bulb in a wire cage on his head, and no hair at all.

"He's programmed to think that's funny," Webb

Washington said to Watson and Fred Achziger. Then, to the robot, he said, "Let us in."

"Who are they?" the robot said, and raised its finger blaster at Fred Achziger and Watson.

"Special guests for the cartoon show," said Webb Washington.

The robot stepped aside. Webb Washington touched a blue square next to the two red doors with the palm of his hand, and the doors slid apart, revealing an elevator car. "Come on," Webb Washington said. Fred Achziger and Watson traded amazed glances as they followed him inside.

Once in the elevator, Webb Washington said, "Bridge," and the elevator began to rise. From the feel of it, it was rising fast. The vibration of the city was less noticeable, but it was still there.

"Why didn't we have to incapacitate Curly with our whistles?" said Fred Achziger.

"Aw, Curly's kind of a favorite of mine. He's the only robot programmed to laugh at my jokes."

"Can we trust him?" said Fred Achziger.

"He's a robot," said Webb Washington, as if that were an answer.

Fred Achziger frowned and shook his head. But before he could speak, Watson said, "Where are we?"

"This is the private elevator of the Charlieville Planning Commission. It'll take us right to their control room."

"This is a building in Charlieville?"

"Sure. It's the Charlieville City Hall. Bet you

didn't know that under all that carved stone there was an albanium superstructure."

"I never even heard of albanium," said Watson.

Fred Achziger said, "A specialty of the Catalog of Raunchypur. It's harder than steel, lighter than aluminum, and made entirely from processed penguin fat."

The elevator continued to rise. Watson had to swallow more than once to equalize the pressure inside his ears with the falling pressure outside. His stomach did a flip-flop and he felt sick for just a second when the elevator suddenly slowed. Seconds later the elevator stopped, and the doors slid apart.

The three of them looked at each other and then stepped out of the elevator into a small room. Another red elevatorlike door stood opposite them; the walls between the two doors were all windows. Fred Achziger and Webb Washington followed Watson to one of the windows and they looked out.

The sun was rising. Suddenly, Watson was struck by the fact that it hadn't been twenty-four hours since his adventure had begun, but only around twelve. He'd first run into the Planning Commission when he'd gotten home from school at about 4:00 the previous afternoon. He felt as if he'd been running for weeks. Oddly enough, he wasn't tired. Probably because of the excitement, he decided.

If Watson looked only at the town of Charlieville, it appeared much as it always did, except that people were running crazily around the streets. Though he could not hear it, Watson was sure there was a lot of shouting going on. But if he looked beyond the city limits, through great billows of dust, Watson could see the desert moving backward at a terrific speed. Which meant, of course, that Charlieville itself was moving *forward* at terrific speed. If Watson craned his neck against the glass, he could see a dark thickening in the haze up ahead that he guessed was Hampton. "Not much time," Watson said.

"Indeed not," said Fred Achziger.

Webb Washington went to the door opposite the elevator, and pushed a button beneath a sign that said SERVICE. Watson heard a bell ring behind the door.

From a speaker next to the button came a voice that said, "Who is it?"

"It's me. Webb."

"We're busy right now," said the voice. "Can you come back later?"

"This is a Conquer Emergency. I think you ought to hear about it before the inspectors from Pudden-take get here."

The doors slid aside to reveal a room that could have come out of a science-fiction movie. The room was lit only by hundreds of little blinking lights. Each wall was covered with them except in the center of one wall, where there was a gigantic knife-blade switch. At the moment, it was closed.

The five members of the Charlieville Planning

Commission were sitting in big high-backed armchairs hunched over a control panel reading gauges, adjusting dials, and flicking switches. They looked even stranger in the dim flickering light of the room than they had in the sunlight.

Above the control panel, about at eye level, was a bank of TV screens. Some of them showed the view forward, others showed the view back. Some of them showed a stylized representation of Charlieville approaching Hampton, and numbers rapidly changing at the bottoms of the screens. Cross-hairs were centered on the spot where Hampton's Main Street crossed the Hampton city limits.

"Five miles and closing," said one of the members of the Planning Commission.

Without taking his eyes off the screens before him or slowing down his manipulation of his control board, another Planning Commissioner spoke over his shoulder. "What is it, Webb?" he said. "We're awfully busy."

"Have a look at this," Webb Washington said.

A third Planning Commissioner turned, saw Webb Washington and the two others he'd come in with, and cried, "Intruder alert!"

Then three things happened at once. Watson flashed the emergency light on his Captain Conquer ring at the Planning Commissioners. They cried out in pain and surprise as they fell back with their hands before their eyes, temporarily blinded. Meanwhile, Fred Achziger leaped to the knife-blade switch and with a mighty heave pulled it open. Every light and screen in the room went dark. The whine of the motivators began to fall. Watson felt the city slowing. At the same time, Webb Washington tangled the five Commissioners in the loops of rope he drew from the ring Martin Trent had given him.

Keeping the light on, Watson ran forward to help tie the Commissioners up with the rope from his own ring. The work of Watson and Webb Washington was not neat, but the tangles of rope would serve to prevent anyone from closing the knife-blade switch again. The motivators were silent. The vibration had stopped.

"Well, as I used to say at the end of every episode," Webb Washington said, "'So much for that mess'!"

"Not exactly," said a voice behind them.

Watson, Fred Achziger, and Webb Washington turned to see five men, each pointing a blaster at them. Each of the new men wore a black fedora and a long black raincoat. Dark glasses covered the eyes in their pasty white faces.

"Who are you?" said Watson.

Fred Achziger chuckled without humor and said, "If I'm not mistaken, this is the Hampton Planning Commission."

Watson did not have forty pounds of brains in his nose, but he knew that something had to be done if they were going to save the Earth. Watson hoped that his plan for using a bit of information his father had given him would work. He looked at his watch and blurted out, "And right on time, I would say."

"Time for what?" Webb Washington said.

"We can discuss that later," a Charlieville Planning Commissioner said. "Turn on the switch and untie us."

"Yes," said Watson. "Go ahead and turn on the switch. I suppose that Berkowitz has had enough time by now."

"Enough time for what?" a Hampton Planning Commissioner asked.

Watson looked from Webb Washington to Fred Achziger. They looked blankly at him. "Go ahead," said Webb Washington.

"The bomb," Watson said. "The plan was for us to turn off the system long enough for Berkowitz to attach a bomb to the motivators without electrocuting himself. He's had time to do that now. When you turn the system back on, City Hall will explode."

"Taking you with it," one Hampton Planning Commissioner pointed out.

"We are prepared to sacrifice ourselves," Webb Washington said.

"Indeed we are," Fred Achziger said.

"Lies. Throw the switch," said another Hampton Planning Commissioner.

"You don't know these humans like we do," said one of the Charlieville Planning Commission members. "They are unpredictable. The only thing you can be sure of is that they are stubborn."

"Yes," said the Hampton Planning Commissioner. "Just like the humans in Hampton."

"Still," replied the Charlieville Planning Commissioner, "they have a strong instinct of self-preservation."

"That's also true. Throw the switch."

Fred Achziger looked at his watch. "Yes, throw it. You'll be surprised." He nodded grimly at Watson.

Watson nodded back at Fred Achziger, then at Webb Washington. All three of them stuck their fingers into their ears. They watched as a Hampton Commissioner stepped forward and gripped the handle of the knife-blade switch in one hand. He pushed the knife blade home.

Nothing happened. There was no vibration, no whine, no anything. Everybody looked at Watson. He said, "If you were the son of Sherlock Congruent, you'd understand."

The Commissioner who'd worked the knife-blade switch leaped at Watson, grabbed his shirt in both fists and began to shake him. He cried, "Explain immediately!" The Hampton Planning Commissioner was interrupted by the chime that announced the arrival of the elevator.

Emerging from the elevator into the small windowlined room were three little men the color of bananas. Not one of them quite came up to Watson's waist. Over his head, each little man wore a space helmet that looked like a fishbowl filled with shimmering red stuff. Watson suspected that the stuff the men were breathing was almost exactly like something that was not quite the same as cold cherry Jell-O. The men also wore blue shorts but their feet were bare.

Behind them were Berkowitz, Martin Trent, Mr. Congruent and the reinforcements from the Modern Methuselah Rest Home.

In a squeaky voice that came from a box clipped to the waistband of his shorts, one of the little yellow men said, "You are sorry excuses for Puddentakers. These Earthpeople have out-thought you at every turn. There will be a full inquiry back on Puddentake!"

"Who are these guys?" said Watson.

"These," said Berkowitz, "are the inspectors from Puddentake. I warned them that their agents hadn't done their job. They're pretty steamed that the motivators aren't running and that there's no power for the Puddentake Field."

"Yes, indeed." The lead inspector pulled a weapon from a pocket in his shorts. The weapon was thinner and smaller than a blaster, but it had lots more knobs on it. He fired into the control room.

Watson backed away as pale yellow light and a hum filled the control room. The light enveloped everyone and everything in it. Watson tingled all over, but aside from that, the weapon seemed to have no effect on him or on the other Earthpeople. Then he saw that standing and sitting where the various Planning Commissioners had been were little men the color of bananas, each wearing his own pair of blue shorts and a space helmet filled with shimmering red stuff. "Come along," said the lead inspector as he put his weapon away.

Dawdling as if they were about to be punished for getting caught with their hands in the cookie jar, the former Planning Commissioners wriggled out from among the tangled loops of rope—now very loose around their small yellow bodies—and followed the inspectors into the elevator. Before the doors slid shut, the lead inspector shook his finger at the Earthpeople and said, "Don't think that Earth is now safe. We will return soon to make your atmosphere into stuff almost exactly like something that is not quite the same as cold cherry Jell-O. Prepare to meet your doom!" He folded his arms across his yellow chest and the doors slid shut.

Webb Washington laughed uproariously. everyone else was deadly quiet.

Watson said, "What's so funny?"

"I don't know," said Fred Achziger.

Berkowitz shrugged.

At last Webb Washington got enough control of himself to speak. He said, "Puddentakers can be terrible bureaucrats. They officially dither about everything. Considering the time it will take them to make the government studies and formal inquiries, I'd say there's a good chance the Puddentakers will never return." He laughed again.

This time, everyone joined in.

* * * * * * *

They all took the elevator down, but they did not go all the way back to the space under Charlieville. They went only as far as the surface. When they walked out of City Hall, they found that everywhere in Charlieville people were talking excitedly in groups. They were discussing what had happened to the city. No one had an explanation, and there were quite a few arguments.

At last they found the bus in which Berkowitz had driven the reinforcements from the Modern Methuselah Rest Home to the Warehouse of Raunchypur. All the old people piled on, talking and joking like little kids. Martin Trent was the last one to board. He turned and suggested to Fred Achziger, Webb Washington, Watson, and Mr. Congruent that they join the residents of the Modern Methuselah Rest Home for breakfast. Everyone thought Martin Trent's idea was terrific.

Fred Achziger, Webb Washington, Watson, and Mr. Congruent walked the few blocks from City Hall back to the site of the Fishbein Studios, where Fred Achziger had parked his purple Volkswagen. It was exactly as they had left it. Fred Achziger and Watson got into the front. Webb Washington and Mr. Congruent got into the back.

They had been driving for a while when Fred Achziger said, "Though I am a man who has forty pounds of brains in his nose, I still don't understand why you threatened the Planning Commissioners with a bomb when you knew there wasn't any. I also do not understand why the power to the motivators and the Puddentake Field didn't go back on when that Commissioner closed the switch."

"It's very simple," said Watson. He was enjoying knowing more than Fred Achziger for once.

"For a son of Sherlock Congruent, perhaps," said Fred Achziger petulantly.

"Well," said Watson, suddenly feeling a little guilty for taking advantage of Fred Achziger. He couldn't help being the way he was. Maybe he *did* have forty pounds of brains in his nose. Watson went on, "In any case, the answer is this: I knew that very soon the motivators would stop feeding power to the city's wheels and to the Puddentake Field because no one was shoveling Chocolatron into the atomic furnace."

Mr. Congruent said, "Then why did you and Webb and Fred Achziger have to storm the control room?"

"Because I was worried that Charlieville would reach Hampton long before the power failed. Then I thought that if I could get the various Planning Commissioners into an argument about whether there was really a bomb, the atomic furnace would have more time to shut down for lack of fuel."

"Worthy not only of a Congruent," said Fred Achziger, "but of a man who has forty pounds of brains in his nose." Webb Washington and Mr. Congruent agreed.

The bus had already arrived at the Modern Methuselah Rest Home when the purple Volkswagen pulled up. There wasn't space in the dining room for all the residents of the Modern Methuselah Rest Home and their visitors too, so Methuselah had set breakfast up on long tables on the front lawn.

Bowls and platters were lined up down the center of each table. Each bowl and each platter was filled with some different kind of food. Ham and bacon were still bubbling; different kinds of biscuits and rolls had fragrant steam rising from them. There were pancakes, french toast, maple syrup and three kinds of fruit syrup, bagels, cream cheese, thin slices of a kind of orange fish, mountains of butter, hot and cold cereal, both hash browned and french fried potatoes, milk, coffee, and tea. That wasn't all.

Watson inhaled deeply, and realized that he hadn't eaten since Methuselah had fed him and Fred Achziger the night before. Still, he had eaten so much at that time, he was surprised that he was hungry again.

Watson piled up his plate and went to sit with Fred Achziger, Webb Washington, and his father. As he ate Methuselah's wonderful food—including Berkowitz's favorite, blintzes—Watson was able to see the new countryside beyond the Charlieville city limits. People easily made the jump across the narrow chasm between Charlieville and Hampton.

Mr. Congruent shook his head and said, "I don't like to think about how close the Puddentakers came to success."

"Fortunately," said Fred Achziger after swallowing a mouthful of food, "'close' counts only in quoits."

"I heard it was horseshoes," said Watson.

Fred Achziger looked at Watson, eyebrows raised. Then he shrugged. "Yes, horseshoes too, I suppose," he said.

"The desert is beautiful," said Mr. Congruent.

"Even so, we will have to file an environmental impact statement," said Fred Achziger. "I'm sure that an entire city cannot be moved without one."

Martin Trent strolled over to them with the very tall man who had opened the door for Watson and Fred Achziger when they'd first visited the Modern Methuselah Rest Home. He was still wearing blue jeans and rainbow suspenders. "Folks," Martin Trent said, "I want you all to meet Harve Fishbein."

"The Harve Fishbein of Fishbein Studios?" said Watson with amazement.

"That's me," said the tall thin man. He put his thumbs under his suspenders and smiled.

"I thought I recognized you," said Fred Achziger. "How are you? Why didn't you say something before?"

"I'm fine. I've been fine for years, since I retired to the Rest Home. I thought I recognized you too, but I didn't know what you wanted when you came to the door, so I kept quiet about who I was. I didn't want to make any more TV shows. How are you, Webb?"

"Better than I've been in years."

"You feel up to making a Captain Conquer movie?"

"What?" said everyone together.

"Sure," said Harve Fishbein. "If I'd had this idea before I would have thought I was crazy. But now, I've seen Captain Conquer in action. And I've seen that he is not only still popular, but he is a force for good in our time. It's not too late for other people to find that out too."

Harve Fishbein and Webb Washington walked off under the trees to talk about the new project.

Looking after them, Watson said, "We'd better call Alvin Algae, Webb Washington's agent. He'll want to be in on the negotiations."

"No need," said Fred Achziger. "I am Webb Washington's new agent. Who better to represent him than a man with forty pounds of brains in his nose?"

Watson and Mr. Congruent both agreed that no one would be better.

Martin Trent nodded and said, "Well, 'So much for that mess'!"

ABOUT THE AUTHOR

MEL GILDEN is the author of many children's books, some of which received rave reviews in such places as *School Library Journal* and *Booklist*. His multi-part stories for children appeared frequently in the *Los Angeles Times*. His popular novels and short stories for grown-ups have also received good reviews in the *Washington Post* and other publications. (See new publications under his name at the Kindle Store of Amazon.com, and his website at www.melgilden.com.)

Licensed properties include adaptations of feature films, and of TV shows such as *Star Trek*, *Beverly Hills 90210*, and *NASCAR Racers*. He has also written books based on video games, and has penned original stories based in the *Star Trek* universe. His short stories have appeared in many original and reprint anthologies.

He has written cartoons for TV, has developed new shows, and was assistant story editor for the DIC television production of *The Real Ghostbusters*. He consulted at Disney and Universal, helping develop theme park attractions. Gilden also spent five years as co-host of the science-fiction interview show, *Hour-25*, on KPFK radio in Los Angeles.

Gilden lectures to school and library groups, and has been known to teach fiction writing. He lives in Los Angeles, California, where the debris meets the sea, and still hopes to be an astronaut when he grows up.

www.ingramcontent.com/pod-product-compliance
Lightning Source LLC
Chambersburg PA
CBHW020128180626
46810CB00004B/1452